GARETH P. JONES

SPACE CRIME CONSPIRACY

BLOOMSBURY

LONDON BERLIN NEW YORK

Bloomsbury Publishing, London, Berlin and New York

First published in Great Britain in July 2010 by Bloomsbury Publishing Plc
36 Soho Square, London, W1D 3QY

A CIP catalogue record of this book is available from the British Library

ISBN 978 0 7475 9981 4

FSC
Mixed Sources
Product group from well-managed
forests and other controlled sources
Cert no. SGS - COC - 2061
www.fsc.org
© 1996 Forest Stewardship Council

Typeset by Dorchester Typesetting Group Ltd
Printed in Great Britain by Clays Ltd, St Ives Plc, Bungay, Suffolk

1 3 5 7 9 10 8 6 4 2

www.bloomsbury.com

For Lisa,
but also for my brother Adam and his girls,
Dawn, Hazel and Fern

PART ONE

Stanley sits down on the hard plastic chair opposite Detective Inspector Lockett. There is a video camera pointing at them. A younger policeman called PC Ryan stands in the corner. Stanley thinks that DI Lockett has kind eyes, but PC Ryan makes him nervous because he keeps looking at him oddly. Lockett smiles sympathetically and says, 'I need to ask you some questions, Stanley. I need to know where you've been for the last seven days.'

'I already told you. I was in space,' replies Stanley.

PC Ryan lets out a snort of laughter.

DI Lockett throws him a stern look then turns back to Stanley. 'The officer who picked you up said you were covered in a kind of white dust. Why?'

'It was ether dust. You get covered in it after teleportation. It's harmless, but it gets everywhere and you end up picking it out of your belly button for weeks afterwards.'

'Where did you get your jacket from?' Stanley is wearing a navy blue military jacket made out of a material she has not seen before.

'General P'Tang gave it to me.'

'Whereabouts does this General P'Tang live?'

'On the Goodship Gusto.'

'In space?'

'Yes, on the other side of the universe.'

'You've only been away for a week. Wouldn't it take longer than that to go that far?'

'I went through cutspace.'

'Cutspace?'

'It's a seven-dimensional universe that runs alongside our own four-dimensional one and allows you to travel millions of light years in a fraction of the time. Professor NomVeber discovered how to use it. Before that, only steppers could go through. Hal is a stepper. He's the cook on the Black Horizon. That's Captain Flaid's ship. He was the leader of the Marauding Picaroons, which are kind of space pirates with heads like birds . . .'

Lockett turns to PC Ryan and says, 'Do you want to sit down, constable? This may take a while.'

'No, ma'am. I'm fine, thank you,' he replies.

'Suit yourself.' Lockett fixes her gaze on Stanley. 'Now, Stanley, people have been very worried since you vanished. I need you to tell me the truth.'

'What people?' asks Stanley. He is surprised how angry he sounds.

'Well, your brother for one.'

'Doug's my half-brother, and he doesn't care where I've been as long as I don't cause him any grief.'

'I'm sure that's not true. And what about your friends at school?' she says.

'I haven't got any friends,' says Stanley glumly.

'What about . . . ? What's the name of that American boy who made the appeal on TV, constable?' asks Lockett.

'Lance Martin,' answers PC Ryan.

It comes as no surprise to Stanley that Lance used his disappearance to get on TV.

'That's the one – nice boy, good talker,' says Lockett. 'He made a most heartfelt appeal for your safe return.'

'He's the reason I don't have any friends,' replies Stanley. A few weeks ago Stanley would have described Lance as his worst enemy. Now there are more worthy contenders for that title.

'Stanley, I don't think you realise how serious this is. Please, starting from the beginning, tell me where you've been.'

ONE WEEK EARLIER

'You're off the rails, that's what you are'

The jukebox was playing a sad song about lost love as Stanley pushed open the heavy wooden door to the Castle and greeted the regulars.

'Evening, Stanley,' said Old Bill, from his usual seat by the fireplace.

'Wotcha, mate,' said Young Bill, who was standing by the fruit machine.

'Hello, young man,' said Gullible George, who was sitting on a stool by the bar.

Stanley had lived above the pub all his life. The squeaky sign outside his bedroom window showed a picture of a turret and a drawbridge, but in reality there was nothing castle-like about the place. Sometimes it felt more like a prison, with his half-brother Doug as the jailer and the regulars as fellow inmates, albeit ones with no desire to escape.

'Where's Doug?' asked Stanley.

'In the cellar, changing barrels,' replied Young Bill. 'Good day at school?'

'Brilliant – I got a science prize, scored the winning goal in football and was voted most popular boy in school for the third term running.'

It was a joke he made every day, but Young Bill still laughed and Gullible George still said, 'That's very impressive, Stanley. Well done.'

'Another miserable day, eh?' said Old Bill. 'I don't know why you bother going to that place.'

'He's thirteen, you idiot,' said Young Bill. 'He has to.'

'Thirteen? I was working by then, learning real lessons, hard lessons, lessons in life. They don't teach you things like that at school,' said Old Bill.

'And what lessons did you learn sweeping up hair in a barber's shop?' asked Young Bill.

'I haven't always been a barber,' replied Old Bill. 'I've seen things that would make your hair curl.'

'Yeah, they're called curling tongs,' said Young Bill, winking at Stanley.

With his parents gone and only Doug to look after him, the regulars were the nearest thing Stanley had to a family. He liked sharing a joke with Young Bill, often at George's expense. Old Bill would offer advice and give him and Doug free haircuts in return for an occasional pint and packet of crisps.

Doug emerged from the cellar door. 'Oh, back now, are you?' he said. He was in a bad mood, but this was nothing new. Doug had been in a bad mood for as long as Stanley could remember. He was always complaining that business was slow, or that it was unfair that he had to look after Stanley.

'You been up to no good again?' he asked accusingly.

'No,' said Stanley.

'Tell him about your science prize,' said Gullible George.

'Don't lie to me. You've been up to something.'

'I'm not lying. I don't lie,' said Stanley.

'Why else are strangers coming in here asking for you?' Doug pulled one of the beer taps and sent foamy beer spluttering into a pint glass.

'What strangers?' asked Stanley.

'There were two of them,' said Young Bill. 'Tall fellas, pasty faces, funny clothes.'

'What did they want?'

'You tell me. But your teacher called me today to say that you've been late every day this term. It's funny, because you always leave here with plenty of time . . . And now these two men turn up.'

'Give him a break, Doug. He's a good kid,' said Old Bill.

'Mind your own business, Bill, unless you want to find yourself barred again,' snarled Doug. 'This orphan's going off the rails.'

'Don't call me that,' said Stanley.

'That's what you are, a kid with no parents.'

'I thought you two were brothers,' said Gullible George.

'We're half-brothers, and my mum's still alive, ain't she?' said Doug. 'When my old man went and remarried I told him no good would come of it. When they died I got lumbered with this little thief.'

'I'm not a thief,' protested Stanley.

'You must have got that from your mum, because my old man was straight up.'

'I didn't get it from anyone because it's not true.'

Doug picked up Gullible George's empty pint glass and refilled it. 'I remember kids like him at school . . . liars and thieves. Do you know where they ended up?'

'Bromley?' asked George.

'Prison,' replied Doug. 'He's heading the same way, I reckon.'

Stanley went upstairs. There were only so many times he could protest his innocence. Doug would never believe him.

The next day, he was sitting on the top deck of the bus on the way to school. Downstairs, the windscreen wipers squeaked rhythmically against the window as they fought a losing battle against the rain. Upstairs, the inside of the windows steamed up with the passengers' stale morning breath. Stanley wiped away the condensation from the window to check that no one from his class was waiting to get on. Even though he caught a later bus these days, there was always the possibility that someone else was running late.

Thankfully there were no school uniforms amongst the herd of grumpy wet commuters at the bus stop. Stanley noticed a short man in a purple suit standing at the back of the queue. Stanley wasn't the only person to have noticed him, but it wasn't his size or odd fashion sense that made him stand out. It was his beard and his bowler hat. They were the wrong way round. His hat was fastened tightly to his chin, while a small pointy beard sprouted from his forehead.

Stanley wondered whether it was one of those TV prank shows where they do something weird and secretly film everyone's reactions to it. When the bus doors opened, everyone lost interest in the man and jostled to get out of the drizzle on to the overcrowded bus.

'Don't push,' shouted the bus driver grumpily.

Stanley looked down to find that the odd little man was staring directly at him. The man waved excitedly and tried to barge his way on to the bus, upsetting a number of people as he did so.

'Stop pushing,' shouted a woman carrying a crying baby.

'Wait your turn,' said a man in front of her.

Stanley felt unnerved by the man's behaviour. What did he want with him? Had he mistaken him for someone else? Stanley had certainly never seen him before. In his experience you tended to remember people with beards on their foreheads and hats on their chins.

'No more passengers,' shouted the disgruntled bus driver, shutting the doors.

The odd man banged on the bus door, but the driver ignored him and pulled away.

Stanley sighed a breath of relief, but the man kept his eyes on him as the bus drove away. Stanley wondered why, of all the people, the man had decided to focus his attention on him. It was attention he could do without. Things were bad enough since Lance Martin's lies had ruined his life.

'If you've done nothing wrong then you have nothing to worry about, do you?'

Before the arrival of Lance Martin, Stanley wasn't exactly swimming in friends but nor was he drowning in enemies. Lance changed all that. He arrived halfway through the first term of Year 8 and was an instant hit. He was good-looking, naturally athletic and spoke with a cool American accent straight out of a movie. As if all that wasn't enough, Lance also liked to boast about his handsome actor dad and enthral the tutor group with stories of films his dad had worked on, big parts he had almost got and film stars he had met.

Around the same time, things started to go missing from the class. To begin with they were small things like exercise books and pens. Next, food from pupils' bags was taken. When someone said their mobile phone had gone and money started to disappear, Ms

Foster addressed the students. She said that if the phone and the other things were handed in, no one would get in trouble. If not, she would be forced to call the police.

Looking back, it should have been obvious that Lance was behind the thefts. His arrival coincided exactly with the first disappearance, but why would anyone suspect the boy who frequently boasted about how rich he was?

Then one Sunday morning Stanley turned a corner near home to see Lance and his dad getting out of a car. Even though they lived in the next road, Stanley had never seen Mr Martin before and was surprised to see that he was some way off how Lance had described him. He was a short, plump, angry-looking man and he was shouting at Lance.

'You wanna go back and live with your mom? Be my guest.'

'At least she's got a real house and at least she's working, unlike you. When did you last get a job?' Lance yelled back.

'The thing is your mom don't want you, Lance. She don't want either of us. Besides, I'll get my break soon.'

'You're an embarrassment, Dad. An out-of-work, overweight, failed actor.'

If Stanley was surprised by the yelling and insults, it was nothing compared to what happened next. Mr Martin raised his hand and slapped Lance in the face, so hard that he sent him to the ground. Lance said nothing. He just stood back up and stared at his father defiantly. His father bent down and picked up something which had fallen from Lance's pocket.

'What's this?' he demanded.

'It's mine.'

'You don't have a cellphone. Where's this from?'

'A friend lent it to me.'

At the moment that Stanley realised it was the stolen phone, Lance turned his head and saw him. Their eyes met. Both knew what had just happened, but nothing was said and Lance followed his dad into his flat.

The next day at school Stanley wasn't sure what he was going to do with the information that he had unintentionally uncovered. He wanted the thefts to stop. He hoped that now Lance had been found out he would return everything as Ms Foster had asked.

But Lance didn't acknowledge him when he came in. Instead he was busy entertaining a group of girls with a story about his dad making a pop video with a famous singer, a story Stanley now knew was, most likely, completely fictitious.

In the afternoon Stanley came in from lunch and saw Lance standing by Ms Foster.

'I'm extremely disappointed to tell you that something else has gone missing,' she announced. 'Lance says that a signed photo of a famous film star has been taken from his bag.'

'It's worth a lot of money. I'll sue the school if you

don't get it back,' insisted Lance.

'Thank you, Lance,' said Ms Foster. 'This has gone too far. Everyone, open your bags and pour the contents on to your desk. If you've done nothing wrong then you have nothing to worry about, do you?'

At first Stanley thought that Lance was just trying to eliminate himself as a suspect. Then he saw a piece of paper flutter out of his own bag and land on his desk. It was a picture of a famous actor with an autograph across the front. Even though Stanley knew that it was probably faked by Lance, the realisation of what had happened hit him instantly. This was compounded when the stolen mobile phone landed next to it.

'You see?' said Lance. 'I told you it was him.'

Stanley tried to protest his innocence, firstly to the tutor group, then privately to the teacher and then again when Doug was forced to close the pub early and come into school. But none of them believed him. Ms Foster thought she was being kind when she gave him a chance to stop stealing and return what he had taken in order to avoid suspension.

The next day the stolen goods reappeared and the thefts stopped, leaving everyone believing that, having been caught, Stanley had given up his life of crime. Stanley's popularity plummeted. He became known as Stealing Stan. His protests of innocence fell on deaf ears. His efforts to implicate Lance looked like churlish attempts to involve the person who had exposed him.

Meanwhile, Lance's lies grew and Stanley was helpless to stop them. Because of his lies, Stanley was now officially the most unpopular person in the tutor group. Because of his lies, Stanley caught a later bus every morning so he didn't have to see anyone he knew on the way to school. He hid in the toilets at the end of the day to avoid seeing anyone on the way home. Because of Lance's lies, life was hell.

'My friends call me Eddie'

'I want you all to think of an experience in your life that has had a big impact on you, something interesting or exciting, and then write about it, describing it as colourfully as possible,' said Ms Foster.

Stanley felt miserable. Nothing had happened to him. Nothing interesting, and certainly nothing exciting.

'So, for me,' continued Ms Foster in her sing-song voice, 'I would choose the first time I ever went on an aeroplane. I remember as the plane came in to land I looked out the window and watched bright sunshine disappear as we flew through the dark clouds, down into the rainy day below them. I realised that even on horrible days the sun was still shining up there. I think about that whenever it's bad weather and it cheers me up. Now, without any discussion, everyone think of your own and write it down.'

The rest of the class set about scribbling away, but Stanley's mind was blank. He had never been on holiday or on an aeroplane or done anything remotely exciting. He had spent his life above a grotty pub, dreaming of a world in which his mum and dad were still alive.

He gazed out of the window, wondering if he should make something up, when he saw the odd little man from the bus stop for the second time. This time he was walking across the football pitch, through a game being played by Year 9, apparently unaware of what was going on around him. He was dressed in the same suit, only now his beard and hat were the right way around.

'Is your mind on the task in hand, Stanley?' asked Ms Foster.

'There's a weird-looking man on the pitch,' said Stanley.

'It must be Stanley's dad, come to collect him from school,' said Lance, causing the rest of the class to titter.

Before the man got any closer, Mr Brooker, the PE teacher, accosted him and led him away.

'Unless this is the most exciting thing that's ever happened to you, I suggest you get back to your writing assignment,' said Ms Foster. 'All of you.'

The rest of the day passed without incident and Stanley had put the man out of his head by the time the final bell rang.

As usual, he hid in the toilets long enough to give Lance Martin time to catch his bus. He checked his watch and decided it was time to go. It was quiet when he finally stepped out of the school gates and there was no one around to witness the odd little man leap out from behind a car and say, 'Ah, Stanley Bound, I presume?'

'Who are you? Why have you been following me? How do you know my name?' asked Stanley, startled by the man's sudden appearance.

The man smiled and raised a hand. 'You'll have to slow down. I only learnt your language this morning.' He spoke very clearly and with no accent. 'My name is Eddington Thelonius Barthsalt Skulk.'

'Your name is what?' said Stanley.

'Yes, it is a mouthful, isn't it? My friends call me Eddie,' said the man.

'Why was your beard on your head before?'

'Sorry about that. I was trying to blend in, but my secretary sent me the file upside down. Here, have a card. It's written in lingomorphic writing so you'll be able to read it.' He pulled out a business card from the pocket of his jacket and handed it to Stanley.

Eddington TB Skulk
First-Class Lawyer
Specialising in Intergalactic Law, Armorian Law,
Pan-Dimensional Litigation
and Criminal Prosecutions

'My number is on the other side,' the man said. 'They'll allow you one call. I suggest you use it to call me.'

Stanley turned the card over in his hand and saw the number.

37484738379839304506067065958282918293286768749393202002198475856874595874945854102929838348485757687687584939392020120843858659409302020393858598494065067072924593938289203029190234321901209210921090

'Isn't that too long for a phone number?' he asked.

The man took the card back and looked at it. 'Oh dear me, yes, you're right. I can't believe I didn't see that. There's an extra zero on the end. How aggravating. That's my secretary's fault. Lovely girl, but no eye for detail.' He took a pen from his inside pocket, crossed out the zero and handed the card back to Stanley.

'Listen, Eddie, or whatever your name is,' said Stanley. 'I don't know what you're talking about. You have the wrong person. I don't need a lawyer.'

'Don't need a lawyer?' said Eddie. 'My dear boy, if

there was ever someone who did need a lawyer, it's you . . . unless you want to spend four consecutive eternities on the prison moon of Trazalca. And believe me, you don't. For the first couple of decades they'll have you peeling stomfrots until your fingers bleed.'

'Did you really just learn English this morning?' asked Stanley.

'Yes. Give me a call after they've arrested you.' Eddie turned to leave.

'Arrested me? But I haven't done anything wrong,' said Stanley.

'Given the details of the case, I'd strongly advise against a plea of not guilty. The AIP will be coming for you shortly. Kevolo's discovered your location, you see. A very good hiding place, this planet. It's pre-contact, isn't it? Who'd think of looking in this far-flung corner of the universe? I understand that this lot haven't travelled any further than that rather pointless moon yet,' said Eddie, pointing at the half-moon in the sky. 'But you must have known the AIP would catch up with you eventually. Luckily for you, I have a man on the inside who was able to give me a head start.'

'What's the AIP?' said Stanley, still wondering whether some grinning TV presenter with a microphone was going to leap out of a bush at any moment and reveal the hidden cameras.

'The Armorian Interplanetary Police, of course,' said Eddie. 'They want to bring you in before you get picked up by a bounty hunter trying to claim the reward, or the League gets their hands on you.'

'Look,' said Stanley, 'I don't know what asylum you just escaped from but I think you should go back there and take whatever medication you need.'

Stanley turned and ran to the bus stop. To his relief, Eddie didn't attempt to follow. Instead he shouted down the road, 'Don't lose my number. You're going to need me, Stanley Bound.'

'Don't worry, I won't let them know you're hiding behind this car, Stanley Bound'

Stanley sat by the upstairs window above the pub. Recently he had started playing a game that involved looking up so that all he could see was sky. He would imagine that he was somewhere else: in a desert, trekking up a mountain or on a boat in the middle of an ocean. Once he had pictured his imaginary surroundings in his head, he would look down in the hope that he had been magically transported there. He knew it was a stupid game. He didn't believe in magic and the game always resulted in the disappointment of seeing that he was still looking out at the same quiet street in south London.

However, this time when he looked down something was different. A circle of utter darkness appeared for the briefest of moments, and two men dressed in long black cloaks with hoods that covered their faces stepped out of it. Without a word or a glance, the two men each drew a staff from under their cloak and walked purposefully towards the pub.

Remembering what Eddie had said outside the school, Stanley made a speedy decision. He ran to his room, which was at the back, opened the window and climbed out on to the kitchen roof, slid down the slope and clambered down to the backyard.

He pushed open the gate and crept around the side of the pub, crouching down below a window and peeking in as the two cloaked men entered the pub. He was unable to hear what was being said, but he could tell that Old Bill was greeting them and he could see very clearly the look of annoyance on Doug's face. 'Stanley, get down here,' he shouted up the stairs.

Stanley tried to see the men's faces, but they were obscured by their hoods.

'Stanley Bound, you do not want me to have to come and get you,' yelled Doug, starting up the stairs.

Stanley ducked down behind the window. His plan was to wait until Doug came downstairs again and then slip back into the flat the same way he had got out, but he couldn't hear what was going on inside the pub so he raised his head and, to his horror, found two sets of eyes staring at him. Without another thought, Stanley ran.

He had no idea who the men were or what they

wanted with him, but he felt certain of one thing: he could not let them catch him.

The pub door slammed as the two men came out of the pub and took chase. They didn't shout after him, but he could hear their footsteps behind him.

Stanley ran as he had never run before.

He turned a corner, and then another, trying his hardest to lose them. He glanced over his shoulder and, seeing they were momentarily out of sight, he dived to the ground between two parked cars and waited.

Looking under one of the cars he could see the feet of the two cloaked men come around the corner. He remained crouched down, his heart pounding. As the men drew level with him he edged around to the street side of the car.

'Hello, Stanley. What are you doing crawling around in the road?' said a familiar voice behind him.

Stanley turned to see Lance Martin.

'Please, Lance, be quiet, please . . .' he whispered desperately.

Lance glanced up and spotted the two men, 'Oh, I see,' he said loudly. 'You're hiding from these two guys, are you? Don't worry, I won't let them know you're hiding behind this car, Stanley Bound.'

Cursing him, Stanley ran full pelt back up the road, the men close behind. He felt one of them grab at his coat, but he wriggled free and ran across the road, narrowly avoiding being hit by a pizza delivery bike that whizzed past. This gave him a little distance from the two men, but he was growing tired.

He turned another corner and saw that one of the men had somehow got in front of him. The cloaked figure stood on the other side of the road, with one hand on his staff. Stanley looked over his shoulder and saw the other man behind him. He was surrounded.

Then, as if from nowhere, a police car screeched to a halt in front of him. The door swung open and a voice said, 'In you get.'

Stanley jumped in and slammed the door shut. The policeman in the driver's seat put his foot down and the car accelerated away. Stanley turned around in his seat and saw that the two cloaked figures were standing in the road, staring after the car.

'This isn't the way to the station'

'Thank you,' Stanley said to the policeman.

'No need to thank me. I'm just doing my job.'

'Do you know who those men are?'

'What men?'

'The men chasing me – the ones you rescued me from.'

'Nope, must have missed them, sorry. I'm Officer Grogun.'

'Are you taking me home now?' asked Stanley.

'I'll have to take you down the station before I do anything.'

'What about the men?'

Stanley noticed for the first time that the policeman was quite badly shaven. He had a thick covering of stubble on his face and a small silver earring in the ear that Stanley could see. 'Not my concern, I'm afraid.' He changed gear as he turned a corner and headed up a steep hill.

'This isn't the way to the station,' said Stanley.

'It's a short cut.' Officer Grogun grinned at Stanley and he realised that, since they had been talking, the policeman's stubble had grown into straggly whiskers and they weren't confined to his chin. Hairs appeared to be sprouting from his cheeks and forehead too.

'What's happening to your face?' said Stanley.

Officer Grogun put a hand to his chin and Stanley saw that the back of his hand was covered in hair as well. 'Oh good, it's growing back. I was worried that it wouldn't. That happened to my Uncle Walt. He shaved his face once for a bet and it never came back. He was a laughing stock.'

'Who are you?' said Stanley.

'I told you – I'm Officer Grogun of the Armorian Interplanetary Police.' He showed his badge.

Stanley felt a wave of panic rush through him. He tried the door but it was locked. Officer Grogun stopped the car at the top of the hill. It was a quiet residential road with a view of London in front of them.

'Ah, now, ain't that pretty?' said Officer Grogun.

'Let me out,' said Stanley, still struggling with the door.

'You've been very well behaved so far, Stanley Bound. Don't start causing trouble now.'

'How do you know my name?' asked Stanley.

Officer Grogun smiled. 'Everyone knows your name. Now, if I were you, I'd take a good look. It may be your last chance.' He pressed the button on the dashboard that would normally have turned on the hazard lights. Stanley watched in amazement as a circle of darkness appeared in front of them, just like the one out of which the cloaked men had appeared.

'I suggest you hold tight. There appears to be some pan-dimensional turbulence in this sector of the cutspace entryspot at the moment.'

'What does that mean?' asked Stanley.

'It might get a little bumpy,' replied Officer Grogun, whose face was now completely covered with hair.

He put his foot down on the accelerator and Stanley heard the wheels spin. The car lurched forward and drove into the darkness.

'There's not much point denying it. You were caught on camera while the speech was being simultaneously broadcast on over two thousand planets'

For a moment Stanley had the strange and deeply unpleasant feeling that someone had turned his internal organs upside down and jiggled them around. The feeling passed and Stanley opened his eyes.

London had gone.

In its place were swirling pastel colours and strips of white cloud making constantly shifting patterns and shapes. Stanley had never experienced such silence before. Where he lived there was always noise, but here there was nothing, no engine sound from the car, no distant rumble of traffic, no police sirens or car alarms, no music from the pub jukebox, no wind rustling the leaves on the trees, no aeroplanes overhead. Nothing but the silent colours.

'Where are we?' he asked.

'We've jumped into cutspace. The autopilot will get us to the Bucket in . . .' Officer Grogun peered at the speedometer. 'I think it'll be a couple of hours, but they made this ship specially to blend in with that planet you were hiding on and I've lost the instructions.'

'What are you going to do with me?' asked Stanley.

'What do you think? You're under arrest.'

'Under arrest?'

'Blast. Having to concentrate on getting this silly language of yours right, I completely forgot to read you your rights. Don't tell Commander Kevolo. He'll put me back on refuse duty. Here, lend me your ear.'

'What?'

Officer Grogun grabbed Stanley's ear with a hairy hand, pulled on the lobe and drew a large gun from the glove compartment.

'Get off me,' said Stanley, struggling to get free from his grip.

'Hold still.' Officer Grogun pushed the gun against Stanley's earlobe and pulled the trigger.

'Ow!' shouted Stanley, grabbing his ear and feeling what had caused him the sudden burst of pain. There was something hard in his ear. He looked at it in the rearview mirror and saw a small silver stud in his reddening lobe.

When Officer Grogun next spoke Stanley heard two different sounds. One was a growling noise that came from Officer Grogun's throat, the second was a voice that spoke the words: 'That's better.'

'What have you done to me?' asked Stanley.

'It's a universal translator. It means that you can understand anyone, no matter what language they use, and it means that I don't have to continue speaking that ridiculous language they use on that planet you were on.'

'You can't just go jabbing holes in people's ears without asking.'

'Oh, quit moaning. Everyone's got one.' Officer Grogun pulled back his hair to show Stanley his own identical shiny stud. 'Now, let's get on with this, shall we?' He cleared his throat, a noise that didn't sound hugely different to his speech. 'Stanley Bound, you are under arrest on suspicion of murder. Anything you say will be recorded and may be used against you in evidence. You have the right to a lawyer under the terms of the Armorian Interplanetary Order Laws.'

'Murder?' Stanley gasped. 'Who am I supposed to have killed?'

'Hah, good one.' Officer Grogun laughed.

'I'm serious. I don't know what I'm supposed to have done.'

'OK, have it your way. You're under arrest for the murder of the Armorian President, the most important man in the universe. You shot President Vorlugenar with an antimatter weapon while he was giving his annual State of the Universe speech last Wednesday.'

'You must have got the wrong person,' said Stanley. 'I've never even been abroad, and I've definitely never heard of President what's-his-name.'

'Vor-lug-e-nar,' pronounced Officer Grogun. 'There's not much point denying it. You were caught on camera while the speech was being simultaneously broadcast on over two thousand planets. Look.'

He tapped a lever to the right of the steering wheel and a windscreen wiper came on. As it went back it left in its wake a TV screen. An elderly man with four arms stood on a podium in front of a star-studded background with some writing behind him that Stanley couldn't understand.

'Why has he got so many arms?'

'I suppose it was so he could shake lots of hands. His predecessor had six sets of lips for kissing babies during election years. Now watch – you're on in a minute.'

President Vorlugenar was mid-speech. '. . . And so I have come to several conclusions regarding Armoria's role in the galaxy today . . .' he was saying when the stars behind him disappeared and a boy holding a gun stepped out from behind the backdrop and pulled the trigger. There was a pop as a bullet hit the president. The president stood for a moment in shock, locking eyes with the boy before fizzling away into nothing.

The boy dropped the gun and vanished back into the darkness.

'The president has been shot,' shouted someone

off-screen. Officer Grogun rewound the footage and paused it on the boy's face.

'It's me,' said Stanley.

'That a confession?' said Officer Grogun.

'No, I mean it looks like me,' said Stanley.

'Does, doesn't it?' Although the boy was wearing clothes that Stanley had never seen, it was undeniably his face. 'We've checked it all: species, eye colour, DNA codes . . . That, my little friend, is you.'

'I don't understand,' said Stanley.

'Explanation mode enabled,' said an electronic voice.

'What was that?' asked Stanley.

'It must be a feature of the car,' said Officer Grogun. 'Oh yes, look, you've activated an infogram. I hate these things.'

From the top of the gearstick a hologram had appeared of a man's head with perfect, tanned skin, immaculate hair and a permanent grin.

'Hi there, my name's Vik Noddle, voted Armoria's Most Endearing Smile five years running, and I'm here to answer any questions you have.'

'I want to know how I'm supposed to have murdered the president when I've never even left my planet.'

'I'm sorry,' said Vik, still grinning. 'I can't answer that question as it involves information I can't access. Do you have any other questions, perhaps about science, history or general knowledge?'

Stanley thought. There was so much he didn't understand, he didn't know where to start. He looked outside the window at the swirling patterns and said, 'Where are we?'

'You're in cutspace,' said Vik.

'That's what *he* said,' said Stanley. 'What is cutspace?'

'Good question. One of my favourites. Well, young man, cutspace is a seven-dimensional universe which runs alongside our conventional four-dimensional universe but, unlike our own, it is not governed by the same principles of space and time. Prior to the discovery of the cutspace drive, the quickest most life forms had managed to travel was ten times the speed of light, which is fine for short hops but far too slow for proper intergalactic travel.'

Suddenly the man's hologram was joined by a woman.

'Talking of travel, Vik,' she said, 'have you ever thought about taking a holiday to the party planet Megaloon?'

'Hey, Dana – no, I haven't,' said Vik. 'Tell me more.'

'These adverts are getting worse,' moaned Officer Grogun.

'Thanks, Vik,' said the woman. 'After an atmospheric entry fee of only twelve thousand Armorian dollars, you won't have to pay a thing.'

'Did you say only twelve thousand Armorian dollars?' said Vik.

'I did, and after that your accommodation, your food and drinks, your nights out will all be free.' The woman smiled and then said very quickly, 'Please note this offer does not include local tax, universal tax, tips or cocktails. Megaloon is not responsible for your personal safety during your stay or your safe return to your planet.'

'Cutspace this, cutspace that. If I had an Armorian dollar for every time someone asked me about cutspace I'd have . . .'

The holographic woman disappeared and Vik Noddle asked, 'Where were we?'

'Cutspace,' replied Stanley.

'That was it. For most of us, cutspace can only be accessed using a spaceship with a cutspace drive. This enables us to stabilise and manipulate the numerous multidimensional factors. It was scientist Professor Nom Veber who invented the cutspace drive, enabling us to use cutspace as a route to distant destinations. Let's go over live to his laboratory on Armoria to ask him to explain it himself.'

On the windscreen a wild-haired man in a white coat appeared, his head hugely out of proportion to his body. He stood with his back turned in a room full of bubbling test tubes and strange models.

'Hello?' said Stanley.

'What now?' said the man, turning around with a bowl of what looked like cereal in his hands.

'Professor NomVeber, this young man would like to learn about cutspace,' said Vik Noddle, grinning.

'Would he indeed?' said the professor grumpily. 'All anyone wants to know about these days is cutspace. What is it? How's it work? How did I come up with the idea for the cutspace drive? I tell you, I wish I never had. That way I'd be able to enjoy my breakfast in peace.'

'Sorry,' said Stanley.

'Professor, your contract with us requires you to explain cutspace to this young man.'

'Cutspace this, cutspace that. If I had an Armorian dollar for every time someone asked me about cutspace I'd have . . .' The professor paused. He grabbed a small electronic device and thumbed in some numbers. He looked up. 'I'd have four million, sixty-two thousand and twenty-one Armorian dollars,' he said.

Vik Noddle's grin seemed to be wearing thin. 'As it is, Professor, you have a contract with Armorian Information Services to answer any questions put to you,' he said.

'Oh very well. You see this bowl of cereal?'

'Yes,' said Stanley.

'Imagine this is the universe. These rather tasty Solar Fruit Twisties are planets and stars, and the milk is the vacuum of space that lies between them. Until I discovered how to use cutspace, we had to swim through the milk to go anywhere.'

'At ten times the speed of light,' said Stanley.

'Exactly. And seeing as the average distance between inhabited planets is around sixty light years, you can imagine it took rather a long time to get anywhere. Now, see this spoon?' Professor NomVeber held it up and dipped it into the bowl. 'Like this spoon, cutspace can dip in and out of the universe. All I had to do was chart which spoons touched which bits of the galaxy and then we could use them to travel great distances at great speed. See?' The professor put a spoonful of cereal into his mouth.

'So we're on a spoon?' said Stanley, feeling a little confused.

'You're riding a seven-dimensional wave that cuts through the universe at speeds inconceivable within the boundaries of our laws of physics.' The professor spat bits of cereal out as he spoke. 'It may or may not be spoon-shaped. Now, please say you understand so I can get back to eating my Solar Fruit Twisties. Since discovering cutspace it's all anyone cares about, and frankly I'm sick to the back teeth of talking about it.'

'I understand,' said Stanley.

'Excellent. Goodbye.' Professor NomVeber disappeared and Vik Noddle said, 'I hope that was helpful. Do you have any other questions?'

'Yes,' said Stanley. 'If you and the professor are both

from Armoria, why do you look so different?'

'That's another excellent question. It's because the professor and I are both children of the Planner.'

'Who's that?'

'Not who. What. The Planner is a machine built several generations ago by Armorian scientists, which enables all us Armorians to realise our full potential. All Armorians visit the Planner in their formative years in order to experience evolution acceleration.'

As Vik spoke there appeared on the screen footage of a machine that looked a lot like a photo booth, except it was black with two white lights at the top, positioned like eyes. And instead of a curtain a door slid open and shut. Each time it did so a teenager stepped out and another stepped in from a long queue at one side. Those going in looked normal, but those coming out had changed. Some were taller. Some were shorter. Some had long arms. Others had bigger heads or tiny hands or a long trunk where their nose had been. When each person was inside the machine there was a flash of light behind the door, and no one came out without some kind of change.

'What's evolution acceleration?' asked Stanley.

'I take it you're familiar with the notion of evolution?' asked Vik.

'Yes. It's how animals change and adapt to their environments over thousands and thousands of years,' said Stanley.

'Ten out of ten.' Vik Noddle pointed his index finger at Stanley and winked. 'The Planner is a highly intelligent supercomputer filled with knowledge gathered from all corners of the known universe and programmed with one basic command: to maintain and improve Armoria's position of dominance in the universe through the accelerated evolution of our race.'

'How can you accelerate evolution?'

'The Planner takes into account physical attributes as well as brain activity. Using sophisticated brain-scanning techniques it can examine us physically and mentally, in essence reading our minds in order to uncover our full potential. By enhancing certain chemicals and improving natural abilities it condenses what would take nature millions of years down to the blink of an eyelid.'

Each time someone stepped out, the machine said in a dispassionate female voice, 'Next component, please.'

'So whatever you're good at, you get better at it?' said Stanley.

'That's right. Whether you are destined to be a politician or a toilet attendant, each Armorian is given the biggest push in the right direction.'

On the screen the Planner spoke in its emotionless voice: 'With accelerated evolution I'll put Armoria at the centre of the galaxy, then at the centre of the universe.'

The footage came to an end and Vik said, 'Currently

the Planner has been taken offline, but I'm sure it will be back in use soon. Our sports players are faster, our singers can sing harmonies on their own and our teachers all have eyes in the back of their head. It's hailed as the best invention in the history of our planet.'

'And this is why the professor's head is so big?' asked Stanley.

'Yes, his already large brain swelled to three times its previous size,' said Vik.

'What about you?' asked Stanley, looking at Vik's tanned skin and immaculate hair.

'As you can tell, my natural confidence and good looks made me ideal for the world of entertainment. Since I stepped out of the Planner I haven't once had to visit the solarium or the hairdresser. I look this good from the moment I wake up till bedtime.'

Stanley laughed. 'So the professor got three times smarter and you got a tan and a haircut?'

'I know.' Vik laughed too. 'Lucky me, yes? Did I mention that I won Armoria's Most Endearing Smile five years in a row?'

'You did,' said Stanley.

'Great. I'll see you next time. Thank you for using the Armorian Information Service,' said Vik, before adding quickly, 'The Armorian Information Service is a copyrighted format. All information is checked, approved and certified by the Armorian Department of Truth. Bye for now.'

The hologram disappeared.

'What about you? Did you go hairy because of the Planner?' asked Stanley.

Grogun snarled. 'The Planner is only used on Armorians. This is all my own hair.'

'Where are you from then?'

'The planet Yerendel. It's a nice place. Lots of shrubs.'

'Why do you work for the Armorian police if you're not from Armoria?'

'My planet got into a big debt with Armoria so every healthy adult Yeren is conscripted into their police.'

'So you never had any choice what to do?'

'I chose to get my planet out of debt. We work for the police so that our children's children won't have to.'

'And all Yeren do this?'

'You do get some rogue elements like my cousin Curlip, who ran off to join the League, but most of us just get on with the job, yes.'

'Restful slumber or brief snooze?'

In spite of the initial excitement of being in space, it wasn't long before Stanley found himself yawning. As the police car made its way through cutspace it vibrated gently, lulling him into a series of unsatisfactory naps, from which he woke himself each time his head nodded forward, until he was awoken properly by something beeping. He opened his eyes and saw a flashing red light.

'We're almost there. You ready for your big entrance?' said Grogun.

'Not really,' yawned Stanley.

Grogun looked at him and said, 'You need some proper sleep.'

'I'm aware of that.'

'Restful slumber or brief snooze?'

'I'm sorry?'

'Or deep sleep?'

'What are you talking about?'

'Here, start off with a doze.'

Grogun flicked the lever that would normally turn the indicators on, and a plastic cup filled with clear liquid dropped out of the dashboard. He handed it to Stanley.

'What is it?' asked Stanley.

'It's liquid sleep. Try it.'

Stanley took the glass and sniffed. It didn't smell of much, but it tasted like cocoa, strawberries and freshly buttered toast. It was cool as it slipped down his throat, and then suddenly there was more energy in his arms and legs. His eyelids felt less heavy. He was more alert. In fact, he felt exactly like he had just had a nice, refreshing doze.

'That's amazing,' he said. 'Can I have another?'

'What would you like?' asked Grogun.

'A good night's sleep,' replied Stanley.

'Coming up.'

This time the glass was bigger and there was almost a pint of the liquid. It tasted of sugar, lemons and strong coffee and each gulp made him feel more refreshed and invigorated.

'That's amazing,' he said.

'Glad you like it. You'll need all the energy you can get. Your arrival is going to be a big occasion,' said

Officer Grogun. 'The commander will want to be there when you're brought in. He loves a good photo opportunity.'

'Photo opportunity?'

'Of course. You're the most famous criminal in the universe. Brace yourself. I'm switching off the auto-pilot. Going in and out of cutspace differs each time, but it's never a nice feeling.' Officer Grogun took control of the steering wheel.

Stanley felt as if his internal organs had remained still while the rest of his body did several loop-the-loops. When he opened his eyes the swirling colours had been replaced with millions of stars in a jet-black sky. This was space as he had always imagined it and even if he was being arrested, it was still an amazing sight.

'You're approaching the Armorian Interplanetary Policing Station. Identify yourself,' said a voice through the radio.

'Come on, read the licence plate. You know who I am,' said Grogun.

'Procedure is that you identify yourself.'

'Oh, all right. This is Officer Grogun, bringing in the suspect Stanley Bound, seeking permission to dock.'

'Permission granted. Please switch off your engines, Officer Grogun. We'll bring you in.'

Grogun took the key out of the ignition. The car turned, bringing a space station into vision.

'The Armorian Interplanetary Policing Station,' said

Officer Grogun. 'The epicentre of all law and order in the galaxy, the headquarters of the largest and most powerful police force in the known universe. We call it the Bucket.'

Stanley could see why. The curved walkway at the top of the enormous cylindrical space station looked like the handle of a huge bucket slowly spinning in space.

'What do you think?' asked Grogun.

'I'm not sure about the colour.'

Presumably in an attempt to hide its ugliness, some bright spark had decided to paint the space station a sickly pastel yellow.

'It's better than it was. When I first started it was pink.' Grogun chuckled.

As they grew closer, Stanley realised just how big it was. Hundreds of smaller ships whizzed around, flying in and out of the station. Unlike Grogun's police car, these gleaming vessels of various shapes and sizes were more how Stanley expected spaceships to look.

Stanley checked his watch. It was half past midnight. He realised that it was only this morning that he had first seen the strange man with the beard on his head. It felt like forever ago. Doug would have rung the last bell and everyone would have left The Castle, unless the regulars had persuaded him to lock the doors so they could stay for a couple more. Or perhaps Stanley's sudden disappearance had changed this routine. Perhaps

Doug had called the police. Would they be searching for him now, asking Doug where his usual hang-outs were, only to find that he had no idea?

They were so close to the station now that it was taking up the whole view, a wall of yellow.

'Can I contact my home?' asked Stanley.

'You'll get your call when you're at the station,' said Officer Grogun.

'My advice is don't say anything'

The police car glided into one of the giant bays and two huge doors closed behind it. They landed inside the hangar with a bump and a skid. Officer Grogun grabbed the steering wheel. They were inside a huge metallic tunnel with sloping sides and green arrows flashing along the ground. The car radio crackled and a voice spoke.

'Officer Grogun, please take the prisoner to arrival bay 271.'

'On my way,' replied the hairy police officer.

The car came to a junction with arrows on the wall. Grogun deftly turned the car up on to the wall in the direction of the arrows, so that what had been the wall became the ground. Stanley put his hand to the top of his half-full glass of sleep, but to his surprise the liquid didn't spill. It didn't even splash.

'Why doesn't it spill?' asked Stanley.

'The station has a multi-gravitational stabiliser so it pulls in different ways, depending on the tunnel. The arrows indicate which way up you need to be,' said Grogun.

'Cool,' said Stanley.

He lifted the glass to take a sip, but Grogun suddenly slammed on the brakes and the liquid splashed out, soaking Stanley's trousers.

Grogun laughed. 'Sorry.'

In front of them was another hairy Yeren officer, sitting on a hovering bike and holding a large sign with a black cross on it. He floated over to Grogun's window. Grogun wound it down.

'Please state your name and destination,' said the officer.

'Officer Grogun. I'm going to arrival bay 271 to deliver this criminal.'

'Please take the western tunnel diversion. This is a restricted area.'

Grogun wound the window back up and headed off in a new direction. 'They're always changing things around in this place. Sometimes I think it's just because they haven't got anything better to do.'

For a few minutes they drove in silence.

'You ready for your big moment then?' said Officer Grogun.

'Big moment? I'm being arrested,' said Stanley.

'Yes, but you're no ordinary criminal.'

A set of doors had opened and they drove slowly into a high-ceilinged room. At the end stood a short, portly, official-looking man, flanked by more hairy Yeren officers.

'That's Commander Kevolo,' said Officer Grogun. 'I bet you twenty Armorian dollars that in his speech he mentions the firm hand of the law.'

Opposite them a number of metallic spheres hovered in the air. As Stanley got nearer, cameras and microphones emerged from within the shiny balls.

'Journobots,' said Officer Grogun, by way of explanation. 'They'll all want an interview and a picture.'

Officer Grogun stopped the car and looked at Stanley. 'You ready for this?' he said.

'No.'

Grogun laughed. 'My advice is don't say anything. Let Kevolo do the talking.'

The doors opened and Stanley was greeted by an explosion of flashes and shouts from the journobots, each announcing who they were before asking their questions.

'This is the *Armorian News Network 204*. Where have you been hiding, Stanley Bound?'

'*Mundanian Breakfast News*. Why did you kill the president?'

'*Universe Today*. Are you working with the League?'

'*Galaxy Kitchen.* What did you have for breakfast the morning you killed the president?'

The journobots jostled with each other, tangling up the leads that protruded from their spherical bodies and bashing into each other in their desperation to get a good view of Stanley.

Stanley shielded his eyes from the flashes. He felt an arm land on his shoulders and pull him close. He looked up to see Commander Kevolo. Up close he was large, sweaty, with a pungent aroma exuding from the armpit that he had just pulled Stanley into. He gripped Stanley's arm tightly and spoke quickly out of the side of his mouth.

'Let me do the talking, OK? You might be a big-shot criminal, but when it comes to publicity you're with the big boys now.'

Stanley said nothing. Commander Kevolo addressed the journobots. 'People of the universe, today marks a great day in Armorian justice. Stanley Bound, the murderer of President Vorlugenar, a very dear friend of mine, has been brought to justice, under a carefully devised and excellently executed operation conducted under my close scrutiny. Today the firm hand of the law came down hard on crime.' Commander Kevolo raised a hand and dropped it down on Stanley's shoulder so hard that Stanley felt his legs buckle. 'The biggest challenge in the universe today is from criminals like the Marauding Picaroons, who think themselves above the law. They threaten all our freedoms. Let this be a message to them: no one is above the law.' He finished with a triumphant wave of his fist.

Once again the journobots burst into activity.

'*Armorian Constant News Channel*. When will the trial be?'

'*Mundanian Evening Analysis*. Who will be representing you in court, Stanley?'

'*The Intergalactic Fashion Channel*. Stanley Bound, where did you get those shoes? They're fabulous.'

Commander Kevolo held up a hand. 'Thank you, everyone. The press conference is now over. Officer Grogun, take Stanley to the incident room and find him a cell.'

'Space pirates, looters – and Flaid's the worst of them all'

Stepping through a door at the far end of the holding bay where the press conference had been, the incident room Stanley entered now reminded him of those he had seen on TV cop shows. There were rows of messy desks, maps, charts and posters on the walls and countless policemen either sitting at the desks or busily walking between them. Even the computers looked like those on Earth. It was the officers themselves who were the biggest difference. Most were Yeren like Grogun, but around the edge of the room, in private glass offices and smarter uniforms, were humanoid officers, who, judging by the number of extra limbs, eyes and heads, were Armorian.

Most were too preoccupied to pay Stanley any attention as Officer Grogun led him through the room, but a couple of the other Yeren officers waved or shouted congratulations to Grogun.

'Have a seat while I find a cell for you.' Grogun pointed at a bench and sat down at a nearby desk.

Among the charts and maps on the walls, Stanley saw a great many wanted posters. Some faces looked human, but others were distinctly more alien. A few were barely even identifiable as faces, looking more like malformed hands, purple blobs or bits of wood. He found his eyes drawn to one that appeared to be a large parrot's head, with grubby, dishevelled blue and yellow feathers and a black bandanna above dark ruthless eyes.

'Captain Flaid.'

Stanley turned to find a small blue creature resembling a hairless chimpanzee, but with eight fingers on each hand and huge saucer-like ears. It was busy trying to crack a large nut-like object.

'Er . . . Pleased to meet you,' said Stanley.

'Not me. In the poster . . . the featherhead. That's Captain Flaid, the leader of the Marauding Picaroons.'

'Commander Kevolo mentioned them. Who are they?'

'Space pirates, looters – and Flaid's the worst of them all. That's why there's such a high reward for his capture. Fifty billion Armorian Dollars – dead or alive. There aren't many things I wouldn't do for that kind of money, but trying to bring Flaid in is one of them. He'd cut your throat just to see what colour your blood was.'

Officer Grogun swung round in his chair. 'Hey, Boosky, leave my prisoner alone.'

'We're only talking. There's no law against that, is there?'

'Depends what you're saying. Don't go giving him any ideas.' Grogun returned to his computer.

Boosky successfully cracked the large nut and threw it into his mouth. 'Talking of rewards, yours wasn't bad.'

'Mine?'

'Yeah, look.' Boosky pointed out a poster with a picture of Stanley on it. Or at least it looked like him, because it was taken from the footage of the president's murder. Below was writing in a language that Stanley didn't understand.

Boosky let out an impressed whistle. 'Twenty-five billion for anyone who brings you in alive. It's a shame that it don't count if you work for the AIP, eh, Grogey?'

'As soon as I've done this, you and me are going to take a look at the new high-security solitary confinement cells.'

'I've seen them. Last time they put me in after breakfast. I was out before lunch.' Boosky turned back to Stanley. 'So why did you do it?'

'I didn't do anything. They've got the wrong person.'

Boosky laughed. 'Sure. There are forty-six thousand prison cells on the Bucket, and every single one of those prisoners is the wrong person too. Even I'm the wrong person, and believe me, I've broken laws that haven't even been written yet.'

'What did you do?'

'He's a thief,' said Grogun, without turning his head, still tapping repeatedly on his keyboard. 'How many consecutive life sentences you serving now?'

'Twenty-seven,' said Boosky.

Grogun swore at his computer.

'But they just let you wander around?' said Stanley.

'Oh, they try locking me up every so often, but you see, getting out is what I'm good at. There's no lock in the world that Boosky Retch can't break. Between you and me, I think they like having me around.'

'The only time you're useful is when you're ratting out your friends,' said Grogun.

'Aw. So you do appreciate me, Grogey,' said Boosky.

'You got no morals, Retch,' snarled Grogun. 'You'd betray your own mother for a packet of astro-nuts.'

'You don't know my mother. I got a lot more than that when I shopped her.'

'But if you can pick any lock, why don't you escape?' Stanley lowered his voice.

'Because they've tagged me, see?' Boosky stuck his tongue out and Stanley saw a small silver stud attached to it. 'I get out of Armorian jurisdiction, they set this thing off and Boosky goes KABOOMSKY! Still, I'll find a way. I'm smarter than these apes and I know more about Armorian law than any of them, and I tell you what – before he starts asking you questions, you want to demand your phone call.'

'My phone call?'

'Yeah, you've got the right to one call. Hey, Grogun, how about letting the kid have his one call?' said Boosky, cracking another nut.

'Use the booth,' replied Grogun, still preoccupied with the computer in front of him. 'And, kid, I'd keep an eye on your valuables with Retch around, if I were you.'

'Ignore him. Go ahead.' Boosky held the door open to a booth by the wall and Stanley entered.

In front of him was a row of buttons with symbols on, but none of them looked anything like numbers. 'Can I call Earth on this?' asked Stanley.

'You can call whoever you want as long as you've got the number,' said Boosky. 'But if I were you, I wouldn't waste your call on anyone but a lawyer. You got a lawyer, right?'

Grogun appeared behind him and grabbed him by his ears.

'Oww,' complained Boosky.

'Leave him alone,' snarled Grogun, throwing Boosky out of the way. 'You call who you want, but he's right, you are going to need a lawyer.'

The door swung shut and Stanley pulled out Eddie's card from his back pocket. He flipped it over and saw that the rows of numbers on the back had changed and now matched the symbols in front of him. By the time he had finished dialling the number, his fingertips felt sore. After a couple of rings, a hologram of a woman's head appeared.

'You're through to Eddington Thelonius Barthsalt Skulk's office. How may I assist you?' she said with a professional smile.

'I'd like to speak to Eddie Skulk,' said Stanley.

'And your name is?'

'Stanley Bound.'

'One moment, please.'

The woman's head was replaced by Eddie's. His beard was gone, but the bowler hat was still on his head.

'Stanley Bound, good to hear from you. I see you're calling from the Bucket, so unless you're applying for the AIP police academy, I'm assuming you've been arrested,' joked Eddie.

'Don't sound so happy about it.'

'I saw your press conference on the news. I thought you looked rather good. Kevolo was as self-congratulatory as ever. Can I assume you want me to act as your lawyer?'

'I suppose so.'

'Good. Please follow these instructions. Do not answer any questions until I arrive. Do not write anything down. You have the right to be taken to a cell and held without being charged until I am present for your interview. I should be with you by tomorrow evening.'

'What should I do until then?'

'Do? You shouldn't do anything. You should do exactly nothing until I arrive. You're in an extremely serious situation. Mistakes at this stage could cost you your freedom and even your life. The death penalty still exists for presidential assassination. Do you understand?'

'Do I understand? Well, no,' Stanley shouted. He had had enough. 'I don't understand anything. I don't understand why I'm here. I don't understand how I'm supposed to have killed someone I've never heard of. I don't understand how this morning no one knew who I was but now I'm stuck in a room full of weird hairy alien policemen, in a space station that smells of cabbage and farts.'

Eddie laughed. 'Don't worry. Just keep a low profile until I see you tomorrow,' he said. 'You don't want to be getting on the wrong side of those officers. OK?'

The hologram disappeared and Stanley stepped out of the booth. The whole of the incident room had fallen silent and every AIP officer was now staring at him.

'They're not soundproofed, those booths, you know,' said Boosky.

'Right, Mr Popular, I've found you a cell,' said Grogun. 'Let's get you in there before you get torn apart by one of these weird hairy alien policemen, shall we?'

'Me Stanley. You freaky talking mushroom thing in my stew'

Grogun opened the door to the prison cell and pushed Stanley inside. The room was empty except for a hard metal bench and a small TV in the corner.

'Someone will be round in a while with some food,' said Grogun.

Stanley noticed a hole in the floor at the far side of the room. 'What's that for?' he asked.

Grogun laughed. 'That's for your waste.'

'What? Like food I don't eat?'

'Yeah, and the food that you do.' Grogun laughed and slammed the door shut.

Stanley walked to the hole and looked down. The smell that hit him as he leaned over it almost knocked him backwards. He steadied himself and sat down on the bench. He felt utterly miserable. He tried to remind himself that he was in space and that this should be exciting. But it didn't feel exciting. It felt like being imprisoned in an uncomfortable, smelly, windowless room.

He checked his wrist to see how much time had passed, but his watch had gone. 'Boosky,' he muttered angrily.

The TV screen in the corner was showing the news. The newsreader was replaced by footage of Stanley and Commander Kevolo. Stanley found the volume button and turned it up.

'. . . No one is above the law,' concluded Commander Kevolo.

It went back to the studio.

'Commander Jax Kevolo was, of course, referring to his ongoing struggle with the most feared Marauding Picaroon, Captain Flaid, whose ship, the *Black Horizon*, has been responsible for many of the recent attacks. This film from a security camera captures one such raid.'

Grainy footage taken from the corner of a spaceship showed several bird-headed creatures bursting in through a door. There was no sound on the footage but it was clear that, had there been, it would have been the terrified cries and whimpers of the crew.

'The picaroons carry illegal weapons designed for on-board combat,' said the newsreader's voice, as one of them rammed the end of a long stick it was carrying up against the throat of a crew member. The picaroon pulled a trigger and sparks flew from the stick, causing his victim to collapse to the floor. At this point the picaroon noticed the camera. He walked up to it, raised his stick and the picture disappeared.

Stanley turned the TV off. Without a watch he had no way of knowing how long he had been sitting there feeling miserable, when a slit opened at the base of the door and a tray slid inside.

'Grub's up,' said a voice from behind the locked door.

On the tray was some kind of grey stew that looked as unappealing as it smelt.

'What is it?' he shouted at the door.

No one answered.

A movement in Stanley's stomach reminded him that he hadn't eaten for some time and that this was no time to be fussy. He looked back at the stew and noticed a long mushroom with a red and black top. He picked up the tray to get a closer look at it and realised that the mushroom wasn't a part of the stew. It was eating it.

'Hey, get out of it,' said Stanley. 'If you want some food, get your own.'

The mushroom turned around. Underneath its red and black top it had a small face with tiny features. It straightened up and Stanley could make out spindly arms and legs.

'Want some food?' said the mushroom, in a small squeaky voice.

'What do you mean, do I want some? It's mine.'

'Mine?'

'No, mine.'

'What's mine?' asked the mushroom.

'The food,' replied Stanley.

'Yes, but what is this mine?'

'It means it's for me.'

'Who is me?'

Stanley was getting confused, and not just because he had fallen into an argument with a mushroom. 'I'm me. Me Stanley.' He pointed to himself. 'You freaky talking mushroom thing in my stew.'

'This spore is this spore.'

'Spore? Is that your name? Well, Spore, that stew you're standing in is mine, for Stanley. Not for Spore. You understand?'

'This spore understand.'

He stepped out of the stew, wiped his feet on something resembling a slice of bread and jumped off the tray.

'Thank you.' Stanley was so hungry now that he didn't care who had been standing in his dinner. 'How did you get here anyway?'

'This spore climb up there.' The odd little creature pointed at the waste hole at the far side of the room. 'Spores live at bottom, but this spore climb up.'

'Here, you can have it.' Stanley placed the tray back on the floor in front of Spore. However hungry he was, he did care that his dinner had been trodden in by something that had just climbed out of the waste hole.

'But you say food not for this spore. You say stew is mine.'

'Exactly. It's yours. Help yourself.'

While Spore greedily guzzled the stew, Stanley explained how the words 'me' and 'mine' referred to different people depending on who used them.

'So when this spore says me, me means this spore, but when Stanley says me, me means Stanley,' said Spore, dribbling the last of the food down his tiny chin.

'Exactly.'

'This spore learns quickly.'

'Yes, but why do you keep calling yourself this spore? Isn't Spore your name?'

'Spore is what I am. Mother spore. Father spore. Brother spore. They live down below. Except for brother. He gone.' Spore jumped up on to the metal bench with remarkable dexterity and sat down with his twig-like legs dangling off the edge.

'What do you call each other if you've all got the same name?'

'This spore the only speaking spore.'

'How can you speak if no other spores can?'

'Don't know. This spore climb up chute to look

for brother. Brother spore gone missing, you see. After that this spore speak. After that this spore left home. After that this spore met Stanley. After that Stanley give this spore food that wasn't . . . mine. After that, this spore jump up here. After that is happening now.'

'So you never found your brother?'

'No. This spore search everywhere but brother gone.'

'If you're the only speaking one, I think it'd be all right to just call yourself Spore. OK?'

'OK. This spore now just Spore. Spore fast learner, yes?'

'Very fast. How can you even understand me? You haven't got one of those universal translating things.' Stanley showed Spore the stud in his ear.

'Don't know how. It easy for Spore.'

'For me,' Stanley corrected him.

'Easy for you too?'

'No, I mean you should say *it's easy for me.*'

'Lots of things easy for me. Watch.' Spore stood up on his tiptoes then jumped up and somersaulted in mid-air. He landed on his head and bounced back up again. At this point he appeared to lose control. His thin limbs flailed and he cried, 'Whoaaah!' before disappearing down the chute.

Stanley ran to the edge and looked down, but was instantly hit by the smell. He stepped away.

'Spore?' he called.

'Talking to yourself already?' said a voice from behind him.

Stanley turned around to see that the cell door was open and a guard was standing in the doorway.

'Just because there's irrefutable evidence that you've committed the most high-profile murder of the millennium, you shouldn't give up hope'

The uniformed guard was a Yeren like Grogun, only larger and with darker hair.

'Follow me,' he grunted.

Stanley asked where they were going, but the guard only spoke again when they reached another door. 'In there,' he growled.

The room behind the door had a white desk and four white chairs in its centre. On the far side of the desk sat Eddie Skulk, wearing a pink and green striped suit. By his side was another man with a wide-brimmed black hat on his head. He had a large weather-beaten face that was almost human in appearance except for his pale blue skin and his luminous green eyes. The eyes turned purple as he watched Stanley enter the room.

'Thank you, Officer. You may wait outside,' said Eddie.

'I got orders not to let this one out of my sight,' said the guard.

'Yes, but clause 807 of article 1669 of the intergalactic laws for fair imprisonment of a prisoner states that the defendant has the right to a short private interview with his legal team prior to the interrogation. You can stand outside. Thank you.'

The guard growled in annoyance but did as he was told. The door slid shut behind him.

Eddie took his bowler hat off and placed it on the table. 'My secretary found me this to blend in on that pre-contact planet where you were hiding, but I rather like it. How are you, Stanley?' asked Eddie.

'There was this one day last year at school when I was chased by a dog, punched by a boy in the year above me and given detention by a teacher for talking when it wasn't even me. Compared to this, that was a good day,' he replied.

The blue-faced man snorted in what Stanley assumed was a laugh.

'Well, rest assured,' said Eddie, 'you won't be kept here for much longer. I'm sorting out your bail. Dram here will act as your bodyguard and make sure you stay within the confines specified by the terms of the bail.'

'Hi,' said the blue-skinned man, whose eyes had now

turned brown. 'Dram Gurdling, private investigator, at your service.' He had a deep, gravelly voice.

'Dram will be helping me with the investigation too.'

'So you're going to help find out who really killed the president?' asked Stanley.

Eddie and Dram looked at each other. Dram's eyes turned mauve.

'Stanley Bound,' said Eddie, 'all the evidence points to you. You've seen the footage.'

'Well, I know it looks like me, but —'

'It's more than looks,' interrupted Dram. 'That footage enables them to identify your species as well as isolate your specific DNA code. There's no doubt in anyone's mind that it was you.'

'But wouldn't that be the same if it was my twin or something?'

'Do you have a twin?' asked Eddie.

'No.'

'It wouldn't make a difference if you did,' said Dram. 'The analysis is more accurate than that. Everything about it points to you.'

Eddie nodded. 'This is true. Pleading innocent really isn't a good idea.'

'But if you don't even believe me, what's the use of having you as my lawyer?'

'My dear boy,' said Eddie, 'just because there's irrefutable evidence that you've committed the most high-profile murder of the millennium, you shouldn't give up hope. The pan-galactic, trans-planetary legal system is a rich and complex tapestry.'

'And by tapestry he means it's full of loopholes,' added Dram with a wry smirk.

'What kind of loopholes?' asked Stanley.

'Well, take your crime. It was committed on Armoria, meaning you will be tried according to that planet's laws, but as it involved the murder of a global statesman it could also be interpreted as a pan-galactic coup, meaning it would fall under the umbrella of the galaxy-wide political-dispute laws. Then there's your own planet of origin. Everyone has a right to have their own laws taken into consideration.'

'But if the evidence is so strongly against me, will any of this help?'

'It buys us more time to come up with other ways to get you off. Say, for instance, that on your home planet the murder of presidents is considered acceptable behaviour. That would help.'

'It's not,' said Stanley.

'Shame.'

'But I'm not guilty.'

'As your lawyer I have to follow your instructions, but I would advise against using that as a tactic. There's too much proof to the contrary. Deny it and you're making it easy for them. All they have to do is pile on the evidence that you did it. If you come clean then we can get to work on finding some technicality to reduce your sentence.'

'I want a lawyer who believes me.'

Dram's eyes reddened. He leaned forward. 'Hey, kid, no one's going to believe you. You need to get that into your head. But with Eddie arguing your case you got more chance of walking free than with anyone else in the whole damn galaxy.'

'And what exactly are my chances?' asked Stanley.

'What would you say, Eddie?' asked Dram. 'Ten per cent?'

Eddie thought about it, then said, 'Realistically, five.'

'Five per cent chance of getting off?' shouted Stanley.

'Well, come on, face it, kid. That ain't bad, considering what you did,' said Dram.

'I DIDN'T DO IT,' yelled Stanley.

'I hope I'm not interrupting,' said Commander Kevolo, entering the room.

'He says he didn't do it. Fair enough. Shame he hasn't got an alibi though, isn't it?'

'This is a private pre-interrogation consultation. You have no right to be here, Jax,' said Eddie.

'Your time's up, Eddie.' Commander Kevolo walked to the far end of the table and sat down. He had a bag in one hand, which he put down by his feet.

'A lawyer is allowed a warning prior to the termination of the pre-interview consultation as specified in clause 811 of article 1669, third paragraph down . . .'

'Your legal jiggery-pokery might work with the junior cops, Eddie, but not with me. And besides, you're quoting intergalactic law. This case will be tried under Armorian law. Or aren't you so up on our planet's laws?'

Eddie scowled. 'I may not be Armorian, but I know Armorian law better than anyone.'

'Then you'll know that this is being treated as a case of planetary security and so pre-interrogation rights can be cut short. I should also warn you that this interrogation will be recorded and that footage may be used in the trial.'

'Conducting the interrogation yourself, Jax? I thought you were above such things these days,' said Dram.

Commander Kevolo didn't respond to this. Instead he addressed Stanley. 'Stanley Bound, please confirm whether Eddington Skulk will be acting as your lawyer.'

Stanley looked at Eddie, then back at Commander Kevolo. 'I don't seem to have much choice,' he said.

'Skulk, you can stay. Gurdling, you're dismissed.'

Dram Gurdling's eyes turned black. 'I don't work for you no more, Jax. You don't get to dismiss me.'

'The accused is allowed one lawyer in attendance at the interrogation. Not any old ex-cop who decided he could earn more by helping crooks wheedle their way out of trouble than by bringing them to justice.'

'It wasn't just the money.'

'Well, you can leave now,' said Commander Kevolo, 'or do you want me to call a couple of guards to throw you out, moonboy?'

Dram stood up. For a moment Stanley thought he was going to hit Commander Kevolo, but instead he turned and spoke to Stanley. 'Good luck, kid,' he said, before leaving the room.

'Stanley, shall we cut this short? Tell me why you killed the president,' said Commander Kevolo.

'You don't have to answer that,' said Eddie. 'The question is based on a number of unsubstantiated assumptions.'

'Unsubstantiated assumptions?' Commander Kevolo laughed. 'Get Mr Dictionary over there. Stanley, you can listen to your lawyer or we can do this the simple way. Why did you do it? Who are you working for? Is it Quil Tisket or General P'Tang? Or is there some new offshoot of the League that you represent?'

'I've never heard of those people.'

'Come on, don't insult my intelligence. You think we're not aware of the activities of the League?'

'I don't know what you're talking about,' said Stanley. 'I didn't do it.'

Commander Kevolo slammed a palm down on the desk and looked at Eddie. 'Hah, you're going for flat denial, are you?'

'No,' said Eddie. 'I request five more minutes with my client before the interrogation begins.'

'No deal, Skulk. You've had your time. So you're innocent, eh, Stanley? Is that what you're saying?'

'No,' said Eddie.

'Yes,' said Stanley. 'Look, this is stupid. I didn't do it. I'd never even left Earth before you arrested me. And the first I'd heard of President what's-his-face was when

I saw that footage of someone who looked just like me killing him.'

Eddie's head was in his hands.

Commander Kevolo said, 'I see. Then I imagine you have an alibi, someone who can vouch for your where-abouts when it happened.'

'I don't even know when it happened.'

'In Earth time, it was last Wednesday at three twelve in the morning.'

'But that's the middle of the night,' exclaimed Stanley.

'Which means?'

'I was asleep.'

'So no alibi then?' said Commander Kevolo.

'Please, Stanley,' said Eddie. 'As your lawyer I strongly advise that you stop this and listen to me.'

'Oh, give the boy a break,' said Commander Kevolo. 'He says he didn't do it. Fair enough. Shame he hasn't got an alibi though, isn't it?'

'I don't care what you say, I know I didn't do it and I'm not going to say I did. You can't prove I did it, because I know I didn't,' said Stanley.

Commander Kevolo reached into his bag and pulled out a transparent plastic bag, with a gun inside. 'Recognise this?'

'No,' said Stanley honestly.

'This is a Series 12, third-generation, self-cleaning Dashle antimatter blaster, known by those who use it as the Damblaster.'

'I've never even held a normal gun, let alone that thing,' said Stanley.

'We'll see about that.' Commander Kevolo pulled two thin plastic gloves from his pocket and slipped them on before removing the gun from the bag, handling it with great care.

'You've seen the footage. This was the gun dropped at the crime scene. It hasn't been handled since. Please, try it out.' He held the gun for Stanley to take. 'Don't worry, it's not loaded – there would be a red light on the side.'

Stanley looked at Eddie, who shook his head.

'You want to get my fingerprints on it,' said Stanley.

Commander Kevolo laughed. 'Fingerprints? These aren't the Dark Ages, boy. As you know, we already have compelling evidence that you were the one who killed the president. But you see, this version of the Damblaster is fitted with an individualised memory handle.'

'What's that mean?' asked Stanley.

'It means that the handle moulds to the specifications of the individual gun holder,' Eddie answered.

'If you weren't the one holding the gun, the handle will have to adjust when you take it now,' said Commander Kevolo.

'As your lawyer, I strongly advise against taking that gun,' said Eddie.

'You're adamant it wasn't you. Now's the time to

prove it,' said Commander Kevolo.

'Please don't,' warned Eddie.

'I'm innocent.' Stanley reached out a hand and took the gun.

The gun lit up and emitted several beeps. 'Processing individualised memory handle . . .' Stanley barely had a moment to register how comfortable the gun felt in his hand before the electronic voice said, 'No adjustment required.'

'Mine's the purple turtle'

Stanley had been dreaming that he was standing in Ms Foster's English class, reading out a passage from a boring play while the rest of the class ignored him, when he was awoken by the same guard as before, standing over him and shaking him by the shoulder. Looking up at the big hairy face, he realised that this was the first time ever that being awake was actually less believable than the dream from which he had just awoken.

'Come on, you've made bail.' The guard hauled him to his feet and tugged him towards the door.

Stanley rubbed his eyes drowsily and paused in the doorway to look back. 'Spore?' There was no sign of him.

'Stop talking and start walking,' said the guard, pushing Stanley down the corridor.

At the end an Armorian sergeant with three arms was standing by a heavy metal door. His third arm was so well positioned for holding his clipboard that Stanley wondered whether it was possible that the Planner had caused it to grow solely for that purpose.

'Prisoner 1675 for bail release,' said the guard.

The AIP sergeant looked at Stanley. 'Stick out your tongue.'

'Why?' asked Stanley, suspiciously.

'We need to tag you to prevent you leaving Armorian jurisdiction.'

Stanley remembered the stud in Boosky's tongue. 'Can't you put it in my ear like the translating thing?'

'We used to do that, but too many of you were chopping off their ears to avoid being caught. We've found people are more reluctant to lose their tongue. Now, if you want to go through that door, stick out your tongue.'

Stanley stuck out his tongue and felt the cold nozzle of the gun against the top of it. He shut his eyes and braced himself for the pain. But when it came it was more of a shock. At the sudden jabbing sensation he whipped his tongue away.

'There, that wasn't so bad, was it?' said the sergeant.

'Big baby,' said the guard.

Stanley lifted a finger to his mouth and felt a hard stud in it.

The officer read out loud from his clipboard.

'Stanley Bound, the conditions of your bail state that you cannot leave the Z1 sector, you are banned from travelling in cutspace and you must stay with your guardian at all times. Fail to do so and we will activate the tag in your tongue. This will send a powerful electromagnetic surge through your body, which can, in certain life forms, result in headaches and mild irritation followed by death. Do not attempt to remove the tag yourself. It is set with a unique code which must be entered before removal. Failure to do this will cause the aforementioned side effects, including your own demise. Please sign here to show that you agree to these conditions.' He held out the clipboard and a silver pen.

'Why would I agree to that?'

'Because otherwise you'll go back to that cell until your trial.'

Stanley took the pen and signed his name at the bottom of the incomprehensible document.

The officer took the clipboard back with his third arm and pressed a button next to the door, causing it to slide open. On the other side Dram Gurdling was leaning against a wall, his head tilted down so that his hat obscured his face. He looked up and Stanley saw that his eyes were the same shade of light blue as his face.

'He's all yours,' said the sergeant. 'Just make sure you keep him within the boundaries of his bail, moonboy.'

Dram's eyes turned an angry burgundy. 'Come on,

kid. Let's get moving,' he growled.

Stanley followed him down a series of corridors. Dram walked so quickly that it was difficult to keep up.

'Where are we going?'

'To my ship, but we're taking a detour to cut down the number of journobots we meet. Eddie don't want you giving no interviews. Luckily I used to be a cop here so I know a few short cuts.'

They turned a corner and Dram walked smack-bang into a large hairy AIP officer.

'Watch where you're going,' snarled the Yeren.

'Watch who you're telling to watch. I'm going to my ship.'

'Not this way you're not. This is a restricted area.'

Dram turned round and led Stanley back up the corridor.

'How long ago did you say you worked here?' asked Stanley.

Dram's eyes turned pink. 'It's been a while,' he admitted. 'I didn't like the way that Armoria uses the police to protect its own self-interests. And besides, Eddie pays a whole lot better. Hold on . . . Listen.'

Dram held an arm in front of Stanley. With the other hand, he pushed a button on the wall. A door slid open, revealing a utility cupboard. 'Quick. In here.' He pulled Stanley inside and the door closed behind them.

'Why are we . . .'

Dram put a finger to Stanley's lips. 'Journobots,' he

mouthed. On the other side of the door a humming noise grew louder, accompanied by two voices.

'Old Kevolo's a tricksy one. All you ever get is the usual sound bites,' said one.

'I'd still like to ask whether it's true that the Planner didn't have any effect on him as a boy,' said the other.

'Good luck – he never answers that one. Besides, I heard that he's started paying journobots to ask the questions he wants asked.'

'I'd never do that.'

'Depends how much he paid.'

'Of course.'

The voices disappeared round the corner and Dram opened the door.

'Is that true that the Planner didn't work on Commander Kevolo?' asked Stanley, following him out.

'Sometimes it doesn't work on people. No one really knows why.'

'Was it the Planner that turned you blue?'

Dram stopped in his tracks and turned round. 'No. It's only used for mainland Armorians. I'm a moon dweller.'

'Is that why they called you moonboy?'

Dram's eyes turned flame red. 'Don't say that. OK? Even if you're just asking. Don't say it.'

'Sorry.'

They walked in silence for a while, then Dram sighed. 'Those born on Armoria's moon don't get the same rights as the mainlanders. They think they're superior to us. I had to work pretty hard to join the cops, but they still never saw me as an equal.'

'So you left?'

'Enough with the questions. We're here now.'

They had come to another door, identical to all the others and, as far Stanley could tell, unmarked.

'Through there is a hangar where my ship is parked. When I open the door, we're going to make a run. The journobots will be watching all the spaceports, so there's likely to be at least one in there.'

'What's your ship look like?' asked Stanley.

'Mine's the purple turtle.'

'Why's it called that?'

'Because it's purple and it looks like a turtle.' Dram pressed a button and the door slid open. 'Go,' he said.

Stanley set off towards the bright purple ship with a turtle-shaped back and a glass cockpit protruding from the front.

As they neared, three journobots appeared over the top of it.

'Stanley Bound!' called one. '*Z1 Sector News*. Is it true that you're planning to plead not guilty?'

'*Universal Crime Time*. Can you confirm that Eddington Skulk will be acting as your lawyer?'

'*The Salon Channel*. Who cuts your hair?'

Dram led Stanley round the back of the ship and pressed his hand against its surface, causing the curved back of the ship to open and form a ramp. Stanley ran up it with Dram close behind. One of the journobots tried to follow them, but Dram stopped, turned and karate-kicked, sending the journobot spinning backwards, crashing into the other two. The door closed as the journobots bickered angrily with each other.

'Watch where you're going.'

'You shouldn't even be here, hairdresser.'

'I've got as much right to be here as you two.'

'Oh yes, that was a killer question. Well done.'

'My viewers will want to know . . .'

Their voices cut out as the door clicked shut.

'We're on TV'

Stanley climbed into the seat next to Dram while the private detective flicked switches and pressed buttons on the control panel. A row of small TV screens showed charts and technical information about the ship, but Stanley's eyes were drawn to one which showed a newsreader sitting behind a desk with scrolling text at the bottom of the screen in a language he didn't understand. Stanley pressed the screen and the volume came on.

'. . . as we go over live to the scene now.'

Stanley saw himself on the TV. Or rather, he saw the top of his head. He lifted a hand and saw himself do so on the screen. He looked up and saw a journobot hovering outside the ship, its camera pointing at him.

'As you can see, Stanley Bound has been released

on bail and is currently leaving under the guardianship of former Armorian Interplanetary Police Officer, Armorian lunar-born, Dram Gurdling.'

The camera swung to the left to reveal Dram.

'We're on TV,' said Stanley.

Dram looked up and saw the journobot. 'Great. Interactive TV.' He jammed a lever back, lifting the ship off the ground and knocking the journobot sideways.

On the TV screen the footage went blank for a second, then cut back to the studio.

'I'm sorry. We appear to have lost that link,' said the newsreader.

'Good. Now let's get out of here.' Dram turned the ship towards the exit and flew it out of the hangar.

'Lawn Waxy is here in the studio to discuss the latest in this story,' said the newsreader. 'Lawn, there's been a lot of speculation about who Stanley may have been working for. Can you tell us what kind of questions the police might be asking at this point?'

'Thanks,' said a grey-looking man, sitting beside the newsreader. 'Many eyes will be on the Planetary League against Armorian Interstellar Domination, most commonly known as the League. This was set up by two men: Quil Tisket of Therapia and Gustovian General Endal P'Tang. Until recently the League's activities have involved protests and stunts designed to garner support, such as this temporary graffiti on the Armorian sun using lingomorphic writing.'

The picture showed a sun with the words 'IT'S NOT YOUR UNIVERSE' in black writing.

'Apart from these easily repairable acts of solar vandalism, the League has done nothing big until now. However, some say that General P'Tang has recently formed a splinter group favouring more militant tactics. This group is known as the Brotherhood and many are suggesting that they are probable culprits of this assassination.'

'So it's more likely that Stanley Bound is working for this second group?' asked the newsreader.

'So far there has been nothing to suggest a link. Perhaps he was just a disgruntled loner. The question then would be how could he have penetrated the tight security surrounding the president without help?'

'And that's a question we'll be looking at right after these commercials.'

Dram switched off the TV. The ship had reached the edge of the space station. Stanley felt himself being pushed backwards into his seat as they shot out into the starry sky.

'No one takes on the Black Horizon and survives'

They had been travelling through space for some time, moving at ten times the speed of light, which seemed pretty fast to Stanley, who was enjoying the way it made the stars look blurry, but Dram kept grumbling about not being able to jump into cutspace because of Stanley's bail restrictions.

'Before Professor NomVeber discovered cutspace, all space travel was like this. It took years to get anywhere.'

'Where are we going?' asked Stanley.

'I'm taking you to my home on Armoria's moon. It's the nearest place, but it will still take a few days to get there.'

'Have you got anything to eat on board?' asked Stanley, who still hadn't eaten anything since he had left Earth.

'Sure,' replied Dram. He handed him something that looked like a chocolate bar.

Stanley pulled the wrapper off and sniffed the bar. 'What is it?'

'It's a sustenance bar. It's got all the nutrients, vitamins and energy your body needs to keep you going for weeks.'

Stanley took a bite. It was stodgy and tasteless. 'Eurgh.'

Dram laughed. 'You can live on them, but they're no substitute for real food . . .'

However, Stanley suddenly felt much better, as if he had eaten a large meal. He placed the rest of the bar in his pocket and noticed something flashing on the control panel. 'What's that mean?'

'Someone's hailing us,' replied Dram. 'It's probably just a journocraft. I'll see what they want, but I'll only open up one-way communication, otherwise we'll be back on the news again.'

He pressed a button, but instead of a journobot appearing on screen, a large mangy parrot's head stared at them. Its grubby, dishevelled feathers were blue and white with yellow around its neck and a patch of black under its chin. Thin black stripes ran below its bulging eyes, above which it wore a black bandanna. Down one side of its large orange beak was a jagged crack.

Beneath this terrifying head was a man's body, wearing brightly coloured, loose-fitting clothing that looked as if it had long since seen its best days.

'This is bad,' said Dram.

'It's Captain Flaid,' said Stanley, recognising him from the picture in the police station.

'This is real bad,' said Dram.

'Hello there, fellow space travellers. My name is Captain Flaid and your ship has been specially selected by the *Black Horizon* for the looting and pillaging treatment. Please prepare for docking or I'll blast you to smithereens.' Flaid threw back his head and laughed.

'We'll see about that,' muttered Dram. 'Hold tight.' He took the steering stick and turned the ship round. 'Computer, full thrust. We'll outrun them.'

Suddenly the ship rocked violently. The control panel went blank, then came back to life.

'Thrusters hit,' said the computer.

'You OK?' said Dram.

'Yes. What happened?' asked Stanley.

'They knocked out our engines.'

'Sorry about that,' said Flaid on the screen in front of them. 'Was I unclear when I gave you the choice between preparing for docking or being blasted?'

'Sorry, kid. We got no choice,' said Dram.

'Can't we fight back?'

'No one takes on the *Black Horizon* and survives. That thing's armed like seven Armorian contact ships.'

'So we just give up?'

'I don't like it any more than you do, but I got to

protect you, and right now that means letting them walk in and take what they want.'

'Hello?' said Flaid. 'Am I talking to myself? I'm not known for my patience. My violence, yes, but not my patience.'

Dram hit the communication button. 'We've nothing of value on board, but go ahead and dock if you like, Captain Flaid.'

'Thanking you kindly.' Captain Flaid turned his head and cried, 'Marauders, prepare a boarding team.'

The screen went blank.

'It's called an agoniser, lad. Have a guess whys it's called that'

Dram climbed out of the cockpit into the main body of the ship. As Stanley followed, the ship lurched to the side again and he lost his footing.

'They're still firing at us,' he said.

Dram shook his head and helped Stanley back to his feet. 'No, that's the connecting tube from their ship. I'd better open the door. The last thing I want is them blasting it open and leaving a big hole in my turtle. If we get out of this in one piece, I want to be able to fly away in this thing.'

'Do you have a plan?' asked Stanley.

'Try to stay alive.'

'Is that it?'

'What do you suggest? The Marauding Picaroons aren't exactly coming aboard to throw a surprise birthday party for us, are they?'

'You've got a gun, haven't you? Can't you fight them off?' Stanley pointed to the gun that Dram kept in his holster.

'One shot from this would blow a hole in the side of the ship and we'd all have a whole lot more space than we could handle. Just stay close by and keep your mouth shut.'

Dram pressed a button and the door opened, revealing a bright orange glow behind it, out of which appeared three silhouetted figures. As they stepped into the hull of the ship Stanley saw that two of them had large straggly parrot-heads like Captain Flaid. One was red-feathered with blackened cheeks, while the other was green-faced with a bright blue beak. They both wore ragged clothes and red bandannas. The third figure was dressed the same as the others, but his face was that of a teenage human boy and he wore a yellow bandanna above his cold, grey eyes.

All three pirates carried long black sticks, which they waved around threateningly.

'You two, tear the place apart. We wants loot'ns and stealables,' said the red-feathered picaroon.

They set about searching the ship, opening boxes and drawers, rooting through cupboards, without caring about the mess they were creating.

'Doesn't look like there's much for the taking,' said the green-faced one.

The red picaroon pointed his stick at Dram. 'You the cap'n of this here vessel?'

'It's my ship, yes,' replied Dram.

'Pleased to meet you. I'm Conur. These are my colleagues. That's Lory.' Conur pointed at the other picaroon.

'Pleasure to pillage you,' said Lory.

'And this soft-beaked lad is Hal. What you got that's worth havin', then?'

'I told your captain already. We don't have anything of any value.'

Conur pushed his stick into Dram's chest. The picaroon's finger twitched on the trigger. 'You givin' me cheek, cap'n?'

'Just take what you want,' growled Dram, his eyes a deep maroon.

'I see, so you're givin' me permission. What right you got to give me permission to do anythin'?'

Dram stared back angrily but said nothing.

'Leave him alone,' said Stanley.

Conur turned to Stanley. 'Who rattled your cage, little one?' he asked with a sneer.

'Stay quiet, kid,' said Dram out of the side of his mouth.

'They giving us trouble?' asked Lory, the green-feathered picaroon.

'Watch this one.' Conur gesticulated at Dram, then bent down to take a closer look at Stanley.

'What's your name? You look familiar,' he asked.

'My name is . . . it's Lance Martin, sir,' he replied.

'And do you know what this is, Lance Martin?' asked Conur, lifting his stick up to Stanley's face.

'No,' admitted Stanley.

'It's called an agoniser, lad. Have a guess whys it's called that.'

'It causes pain?' guessed Stanley.

The red-feathered bird-headed pirate laughed. 'That'll be right, lad. Pain. Agony. Even death, if I sets it high enough. You want to see how it works?'

'Leave the boy out of this,' said Dram. 'I already said, you can take what you want.'

Conur swung his head back to look at Dram. 'Take? Take?' he squawked. 'I wants to take this boy's life. That all right with you, cap'n?'

'Let's kill 'em both,' said Lory.

'You touch that boy and killing me won't be enough to keep you safe,' snarled Dram, his eyes darkening.

'You threatenin' us?' Lory swung the agoniser at Dram's head but Dram ducked and kicked away his legs. Lory fell, dropping the weapon. Conur lunged at Dram. Dram dodged the attack and elbowed him in the beak. He grabbed the agoniser that Lory had dropped and kicked Conur in the stomach, sending him down.

'Grab his weapon,' shouted Dram.

Stanley reached for the agoniser but felt something

cold against his throat and a hand gripping his chin.

It was the third pirate, the human called Hal.

'Leave it,' he whispered in Stanley's ear.

'Do as he says,' said Dram.

Stanley dropped the agoniser.

'Let's all stay calm,' said Dram. 'Stanley, he's got a volt-dagger held against your throat. Don't do anything rash. Listen, Hal, is that your name? We can sort this out without anyone getting hurt. You don't want your two shipmates to get hurt, do you?' He waved the stick at the two picaroons who were still on the floor.

'Drop your weapon,' said Hal. Stanley could feel his breath on the back of his neck.

Then Stanley felt Hal's grip loosen. In fact, it was as though reality itself was loosening its grip. The scene in front of him whitened, like a camera flash in slow motion. Sound ebbed away. He could see that Dram was speaking but he could no longer hear his words. Sight and sound were replaced by pain. It seared through his body.

He realised what must have happened. Hal must have squeezed the trigger of the volt-dagger. Stanley could think of no other explanation except that what he was experiencing was death. Everything was white. All form had gone. Stanley was alone. He was no more.

PART TWO

'Let's take a break,' says DI Lockett. 'Stanley, do you want something to eat or drink?'

'No, thanks,' replies Stanley.

'Well, I'd like a cup of tea. Are you sure I can't interest you in a biscuit or anything?'

'I'm fine, thank you.'

'OK. We won't be long.' DI Lockett motions to PC Ryan and they leave the room together. The room has a two-way mirror, which enables the two police officers to look in on Stanley, who remains seated behind the desk.

'What do you think?' asks Lockett.

'He's clearly making up these stories instead of telling us what really happened,' PC Ryan replies.

'He doesn't appear to be making it up. And look, he does have a stud in his ear.'

'Well, that proves it. A stud. He must have been to space. It's the only explanation.'

Lockett doesn't like the tone of PC Ryan's voice. 'Sergeant, don't make me remind you that I am your superior officer.'

'Sorry, ma'am, no disrespect intended. It just all seems so incredible. And remember that he said something about a stud in his tongue, but that's not there.'

'Of course not. That was a tag which prevented him from travelling through cutspace and, without cutspace travel, he would have taken years to get back to Earth.'

'Are you feeling all right, ma'am?'

'It just seems like . . . you know, he's telling the truth . . .'

'With respect, ma'am, the boy just told us that he died.'

'No, he said that's what it felt like.'

'But come on . . . talking mushrooms, hairy police officers, parrot-headed pirates . . . Don't say you believe this stuff.'

Lockett knows the room is soundproofed, but she still finds herself worrying about being overheard by Stanley so she steps away from the glass. 'No, I suppose not. What I mean is that he seems to believe it himself. I don't get any sense that he's making it up as he goes along.'

'There you are, then. Delusional. There's a good child psychologist based nearby . . . Do you want me to contact him?'

'Yes, that's a good idea. In the meantime, I'll let him carry on with his story. I think it's helping him to tell it.'

She doesn't admit her real reason for wanting Stanley to continue with his story. She wants to know what happens next.

'Yeah, well, someone had to do it'

For a moment Stanley honestly believed he was dead. What else could it be? He was unable to see anything. He was unable to hear anything. He couldn't feel pain. He couldn't feel pleasure. It was as though he no longer existed at all. Then, in the midst of the mist, he heard a small voice say, 'Me scared.'

A second later, shapes began to materialise out of the blankness, appearing at first like a pencilled drawing before slowly gaining colour and texture. As the scene took shape he realised that the picaroons and Dram had gone and that he wasn't inside the purple turtle any more.

Instead he was in a room full of staring faces. Some were human in appearance. But there was also a Yeren and a couple of blue-faced moon dwellers, as well as aliens that Stanley hadn't encountered before. All of them wore matching navy blue uniforms with gold buttons. At the front of this crowd stood a large man whose uniform was covered in medals. He wore a neat military-looking hat, a thick moustache and large pair of sunglasses that reflected Stanley's own bewildered face.

As Stanley felt the weight of existence return to his body, the group of strangers burst into applause. The man with the moustache stepped forward and grasped Stanley's hand, giving it a firm shake.

'Stanley Bound. It gives me great honour to welcome you aboard the Goodship *Gusto*. I'm General P'Tang, leader of the Brotherhood. You're safe now. You're with friends.'

The crowded room appeared to be some kind of spaceship control deck. Panels of flashing lights, levers, buttons, gauges and screens lined the walls. A curved glass window at the front showed Dram's ship suspended in space, with a much larger ship attached by a connecting tube. The picaroons' ship was as ragged and intimidating as Stanley would have expected, looking like it had been cobbled together from spare parts and then heavily armed with hundreds of ferocious-looking guns and cannons so that it resembled a giant metal porcupine.

'Brothers, take us out of here with haste,' ordered General P'Tang. 'It won't take Captain Flaid long to realise what's happened.'

'What about Dram?' asked Stanley.

'Teleporting uses up a lot of energy. Few ships have enough battery power to teleport more than one person at a time. The battery needs to recharge itself now.'

'But the picaroons will kill him.'

General P'Tang placed a hand on Stanley's shoulder and looked down at him. 'Sacrifices are sometimes as necessary as they are painful.'

'But you can't leave him to die,' protested Stanley.

'You're the priority right now, Stanley. The detective will be able to look after himself.'

'But . . .'

'No more buts. Right, let's get you cleaned up.'

Stanley realised the general was referring to a thin layer of grey-white powder that covered his clothes. 'What is it?'

A girl dressed in the same military uniform as the others said, 'It's ether dust. It's a by-product of the teleporting process. It's harmless, but it does get everywhere. You'll be picking it out of your belly button for weeks.' She was around the same age as Stanley. Her dark brown hair was tied back away from her pale face and like General P'Tang she wore mirrored glasses.

'Stanley Bound, may I introduce my daughter, Jupp.'

'Hi,' said Stanley.

'Stick out your tongue,' said the girl.

'I'm sorry?'

Jupp pulled from her belt what looked like a small gun with pincers at the end of the barrel.

'Please do as I say. We haven't much time.'

Stanley stuck out his tongue.

'Yep, you've been tagged,' she said. 'Hold still, while I remove it for you.'

'But they said it was impossible to remove it without killing me,' protested Stanley.

'It's not impossible. It's simply a matter of finding the correct individualised code, then deactivating it before removing the tag. That's what this does. I invented it myself.'

'There's nothing to worry about. My daughter is an electronics whizz,' said General P'Tang proudly.

'Now give me your tongue.' Jupp grabbed the end of it with one hand and carefully guided the gun's pincers over either side of the tag.

'Ah wah yah lah,' said Stanley,

'Hold still,' ordered Jupp. 'This won't hurt.'

She was wrong. A sudden burst of pain tore through Stanley's mouth. It felt like his tongue was being ripped out. He pulled away and put a hand to it and was relieved to find his tongue was still there and the tag was gone.

'Well done, Jupp,' said General P'Tang. 'I knew it would work.'

'What's that mean?' asked Stanley.

'Well, you were the first tagged prisoner we've

encountered since I invented it,' said Jupp.

'So you could have killed me?'

'It was pretty unlikely, but what's worse? Death or life as an Armorian prisoner?' asked Jupp. Before Stanley could respond she said, 'After all, you've already shown your bravery and devotion to the cause by killing President Vorlugenar, which was totally brilliant, by the way.'

'Brothers, prepare the ship for cutspace entry,' said General P'Tang.

Three crew members sitting at one of the control panels turned around and saluted. 'Yes, General, right away, General,' they said.

'All brothers to their stations,' he barked.

'Why have you brought me here?' asked Stanley, feeling what was, by now, a familiar sensation of utter confusion.

General P'Tang smiled. 'Why? Because your actions have shown you to be one of us. You're a hero, my boy. Now my daughter will take you somewhere to clean up.'

Stanley followed Jupp out of the control room into a busy corridor. She grabbed his hand and pulled him through the crowds of aliens all wearing the same blue uniform. 'Who are you people?' he asked.

'We're the Brotherhood.'

'What is that?'

'We used to be with the League, but Dad had a

falling-out with Quil Tisket because he's all talk and no action. Dad says that the only way to make your voice heard in this universe is to use force, not words. Like you did by killing the Armorian president. Everyone here wished they'd done that. It's so cool. Getting past all that security must have been difficult. I can't imagine how you did it and I'm top of political assassination class. You must be really smart. Not to mention brave.'

Stanley didn't know why he said what he said next. Perhaps it was because Jupp was pretty, had a nice smile and was holding his hand. Or because she looked at him so admiringly when she said that he was smart and brave. Or perhaps he was fed up that no one believed him when he did deny it. Whatever the reason, he replied, 'Yeah, well, someone had to do it.'

'Growing up on a spaceship must be pretty cool though'

Stanley had never been anywhere more crowded than the corridors of the Goodship *Gusto*. They were filled with hundreds of aliens of various shapes and sizes, all apparently heading in different directions. Along one of these bustling corridors, Stanley noticed a row of small doors, about knee height.

'What are those?' he asked.

'Escape pods,' replied Jupp. 'All ships have them. If something goes wrong with the ship, you get in, shut the door behind you and they automatically take you to the nearest habitable planet.'

Stanley bent down and peered through a window in one of the doors. Behind it was a tiny capsule big enough for one person. 'There must be a lot on this ship for all these people.'

'This is all of them,' replied Jupp. 'Dad only designed the ship for me and him, but everyone who joins the Brotherhood comes to live here.'

'So that's why there are so many people on board?'

'Yeah. Dad gives them all jobs too.' They passed four aliens fighting over who got to change a faulty light bulb. 'He says that everyone has the right to work. So there tend to be at least three people for each task.'

'Doesn't that cause problems?'

'Sometimes. The other day there were five people trying to steer the ship and we almost flew into a small moon. It's a good sign though, because it means that the Brotherhood is getting stronger. We'll have enough for an attack soon.'

She stopped at a door.

'This is my room. You can clean off the ether dust here.'

The door opened to reveal a small room. In one corner was a shower. Along one wall was a bed. Above it there was a silver picture frame around a black centre.

'Where's the picture?' asked Stanley.

'You can't see it because you're an overgrounder. It's a picture of my family on Gusto, before our city collapsed.'

'Do you live underground then?'

'We did, yes. Gusto is too near its sun. The surface is too hot and too volatile so we lived underground. Over the centuries our eyes have become more and more accustomed to the dark, so now what seems pitch black to you is bright enough light for me to read by.'

Looking closely at the picture, Stanley could make out faint outlines against the darkness but no details. 'Is that why you wear the dark glasses?'

'Yeah, otherwise it would be too bright. That's what happened when the city caved in. Millions were blinded and couldn't find their way to safety. That's how my mother died.' Jupp's voice wavered.

'I'm sorry,' Stanley said, thinking about his own parents. 'Do you think you'll go back there?'

'Dad says he won't return until he has led the victory over the Armorians.'

'Growing up on a spaceship must be pretty cool though.'

'Yeah, but I still miss how things were. I miss home,' said Jupp.

'Well, I'm never going back to mine,' said Stanley. What had he to miss? No real family and no real friends.

'That's different. People still live on Gusto. I could still go back,' said Jupp. 'You're a wanted criminal. You couldn't go home even if you wanted to.'

'What are you doing in my trousers?'

Before leaving, Jupp showed Stanley how a drawer that pulled out of the wall could be used to clean his clothes, so once she was gone he removed his dirty shirt and placed it inside. He shut the drawer and opened it, as instructed, and was pleased to see the shirt come out clean and smelling fresh. He undid his trousers and was about to put them in too when he remembered that the sustenance bar Dram had given him was still in the pocket. He put his hand in to get it, but came out with just the wrapper. He reached in again and felt something soft and squidgy. It wriggled. Stanley remembered the voice he had heard during the teleportation. 'Spore? Is that you?'

Spore's red and black mushroom top emerged from his right pocket. 'Hello, Stanley.'

'What are you doing in my trousers?'

Spore climbed out of the pocket and up on to the bedside table. 'After you left me the first time me was lonely. Me didn't want to feel like that again so me hid with you.'

'You mean, you've been there since I left the cell?'

'Yes. Me stay quiet, me not want to cause any trouble.'

'They must have counted you as one of my possessions when they teleported me over.'

'Spore not your possession.' He sounded nervous. 'Me not want to be owned by Stanley. Me scared Stanley might take away Spore's life too.'

'I'm not going to hurt you,' said Stanley. 'I haven't killed anyone.'

'But you said to the girl –'

'I know,' he interrupted him. 'I know. I lied.'

'Why you do this?'

'Because . . . I don't know. I suppose because Jupp seemed so impressed by what I'd done. Or what she thinks I've done. No one's ever really been impressed by me like that. So I let her believe what she wanted to believe.'

Spore stopped struggling in Stanley's hand. 'Has Stanley lied to me?'

'No, you can trust me. I won't lie to you. I'm your friend.'

'Spore like to be friends if Stanley not take my life.

Me not had friend before. Stanley is Spore's only friend. Me will trust Stanley.'

'Good. I'm glad you're my friend too.'

While getting clean in the shower, Stanley considered how he would come clean with Jupp. As he did up the buttons on his shirt he was working out what he would say, when the door buzzer sounded.

'Me hide.' Spore leaped into the air and landed inside Stanley's pocket as the door slid open and Jupp entered.

'Hi.' She greeted Stanley with a warm smile.

'Hi, listen . . .' began Stanley, sensing himself redden at the thought of what he had to say.

'Can you tell me on the way? Dad wants to talk to you before we arrive.'

'Arrive where?'

'We're going to Quil Tisket's place on Therapia. Quil's the one Dad started the League with. Dad says he's a great man but he needs to understand that actions are better than words.'

'Why are we going to see him?'

'Dad wants to persuade Quil to join us and wage war against the Armorians. He thinks meeting you will inspire him. There aren't enough of us in the Brotherhood to take on the whole of the AIP, but with Quil and the rest of the League we'd be able to launch an attack, while they haven't got a president to unite them.'

'An attack?'

'Dad will explain it much better. Hurry, we'll be coming out of cutspace soon.' She took his hand and the idea of telling her the truth suddenly seemed less pressing.

She led him back to the bustling bridge of the Goodship *Gusto*. Standing in its centre was General P'Tang. He greeted Stanley with a firm handshake and a powerful slap on the back.

'Well met, Stanley Bound. You look much better. Clean hair and a fresh shirt . . . Only one thing missing.'

'What's that?'

General P'Tang picked up a box from his seat and handed it to Stanley. 'Don't look so worried, Brother Bound. It's a gift.'

Stanley looked at Jupp, who nodded and smiled encouragingly. Stanley opened the box. Inside was a dark blue jacket with gold buttons, identical to those worn by everyone else on the ship.

'Made of one hundred per cent astral goat hair. Only true brothers of the Brotherhood wear these. Now you are one of us. You are equal, as all brothers are equal,' General P'Tang beamed.

'Go on, try it on,' said Jupp.

Stanley took the jacket and slipped his arms through the sleeves. It fitted perfectly.

'I can't wear this,' he protested.

'Nonsense. After all, by what you have done you are

as true a brother as any on this ship. The Armorians have built a wall of terror around our galaxy for many years, but you have knocked away the first brick of that wall. Together, you and I will be able to help convince Quil that now is the time for action, I'm sure of it.'

'No, I can't.'

General P'Tang placed a hand on Stanley's shoulder. 'Let me tell you something about my history, Stanley.'

'I've already told him about the city collapsing,' said Jupp.

General P'Tang carried on regardless. 'Gusto has no great mountains or oceans, but below the surface my people created an underground paradise.'

Jupp raised her eyebrows at Stanley, indicating that she had heard this speech before.

'We Gustovians are great miners and the belly of our home was rich with fuels, food and minerals, which we used to build great cities with architectural splendour and a vibrant culture. And then the Armorians arrived. We were the first inhabited planet they discovered, you know?'

Jupp mouthed along with the next bit of the speech, forcing Stanley to stifle a giggle.

'The Armorians brought great tools, which they shared with us in exchange for resources from our planet, but with this new technology, my ancestors mined deeper and faster than ever before, and soon our fertile planet was a hollow shell. What is more, our own traditions disappeared as my people became enamoured with unnecessary Armorian gadgets.'

Jupp stopped mouthing as her father said with a wobble in his voice, 'The collapse of Porth Methryl was the final straw.'

'Did the Armorians do that too?' asked Stanley.

'Our great capital collapsed because of illegal mining beneath its foundations, mining that would never have been possible without Armorian technology. My wife and millions of others died because of Armoria. Since then, the discovery of cutspace has enabled them to travel further with greater speed and plunder ever more planets. There are many on board this ship who will tell you similar stories.'

Stanley looked around the bridge at the aliens, all wearing the same blue uniform.

'Shortly we shall arrive on Therapia and meet with Quil Tisket. Together we will convince him that now is the time to make a stand. You have shown us this with your brave action, Stanley Bound. Now is the time to fight.'

General P'Tang concluded with a dramatic wave of his fist, which got a rapturous round of applause from everyone on the bridge.

'What say you, Stanley? Will you fight with me?' He offered his hand.

Stanley glanced from face to face, each weird alien

eye focused on him in anticipation, each set of hands, feet, flippers or tentacles applauding him. He swallowed hard then took General P'Tang's hand and said, 'Yes, General, I will fight with you.'

'He seems rather lacking in moral fibre, this one'

As the Goodship *Gusto* came out of cutspace, Stanley experienced the odd sensation that someone was playing table tennis with his eyeballs while nibbling on his toes and rubbing sandpaper on his fingertips. The feeling vanished as the swirling colours that had been on the main screen were replaced by the endless stars of space.

'Set a course for the far side of Therapia,' said General P'Tang.

Three crew members squeezed into one seat squabbled over who got to do this and slowly the ship turned, bringing a large green planet into view.

General P'Tang smiled and turned to Stanley. 'Welcome to the one safe haven in the known universe, the planet of Therapia.'

'Why is it safe?' asked Stanley.

'Because it's outside Armorian jurisdiction. This is the most peaceful place you'll ever encounter.'

'General P'Tang, sir,' said a crew member who had skin like lemon peel.

'What is it?' barked the general.

'Someone's hailing us,' said another two crew members, one resembling a purple-scaled toad and one a large blue beetle.

'Thank you. Let's see who it is. On screen.'

The three crew members fought over the controls until the blue beetle pushed the one with purple scales, who knocked lemon peel skin's elbow against the right button.

Stanley instantly recognised the inside of the ship that appeared on the screen as the police car in which Officer Grogun had arrested him back on Earth, and he didn't need a qualification in spaceship maintenance to see that it was in trouble. The lights on the dashboard were flickering, smoke was pouring out and a small fire had broken out in the passenger seat. Sitting in the driving seat was also something Stanley recognised. It was a small blue eight-fingered chimpanzee with large circular ears. And it was panicking. 'If there's anyone out there, please help. This piece of junk couldn't take the re-entry from cutspace.'

'It's Boosky,' said Stanley.

'Do you know this person?' asked General P'Tang.

'His name's Boosky Retch. He's a thief. I met him when I was on board the Bucket.'

'Well, the battery has recharged enough to teleport him. Shall we bring him aboard?' asked General P'Tang.

Boosky scampered around the inside of the ship, trying to put out the fires that kept springing up.

'I'd like to speak to him first,' said Stanley.

'Communication brothers, open a two-way channel, please.'

The blue beetle pushed the relevant button.

'Hello?' said Boosky. 'Is someone there?'

'Where's my watch?' demanded Stanley.

'Stanley Bound, is that you?' Boosky climbed up close to the camera, so that his nostrils appeared like two hairy caverns on the screen.

'We can teleport you aboard, but I want the watch you stole off me.'

'Stole? You got me all wrong. I never stole no watch off no one.'

'All right, if that's the way you want to play it, I'll leave you to it.'

'No, no, no. I just realised what you mean. You mean this thing?' Boosky pulled Stanley's watch from the glove compartment and held it up. 'I didn't steal it though. The prison guards would have confiscated it if I hadn't looked after it for you.'

'He seems rather lacking in moral fibre, this one,' observed General P'Tang.

'Moral fibre? Who are you people?' asked Boosky.

'This is the Goodship *Gusto*,' replied the general. 'We are the Brotherhood. We are fighting for a universe liberated from the tyrannical oppression of Armoria. What is your cause, Brother Retch?'

Something exploded on the dashboard, causing Boosky to yelp and duck out of view. He raised his head and said, 'Right now, my cause is getting off this ship in one piece. Are you going to help me or not?'

'What do you say, Stanley? You really want us to bring him aboard?' asked General P'Tang.

'We can't let him die,' said Stanley.

General P'Tang nodded sagely and said, 'Brothers, teleport him over.'

On the screen it looked as though Boosky was hastily being rubbed out from his edges by an artist keen to delete his mistake and start again. Once he had disappeared, all that remained where he had stood was his outline in white, which hung in the air for a second before dropping to the floor.

The screen then showed the outside of the police car, which very suddenly exploded into pieces. Amongst the debris that floated past them, Stanley managed to spot the police siren, a spare tyre and an *A-Z* of London.

In the same spot that Stanley had first materialised on the deck, a distinctive silhouette appeared in white.

Then, as though the same artist who had rubbed him out was now redrawing him, Boosky materialised. He looked down at himself, checking all his bits and pieces were intact, and brushed the grey-white dust off his arms.

'Welcome aboard, Brother Retch,' said General P'Tang.

'It's good to be here, General.'

'I'll take that.' Stanley snatched his watch out of Boosky's hand and put it on his wrist. 'How did you escape from the Bucket anyway?'

'How? I'll tell you how. You went missing, that's how,' said Boosky. 'As soon as your signal disappeared, Commander Kevolo went ballistic. He gave the order that everyone drop what they were doing and concentrate on finding you. With everyone looking for you, I grabbed a ship and got out before they noticed I'd gone.'

'But they'll activate your tag and kill you, won't they?'

Boosky stuck his tongue out. The tag was no longer there. 'They were supposed to be putting a new one in, so they took the old one out and I slipped away before they could replace it. What happened to yours? The whole place went crazy when your signal disappeared.'

'I removed it,' said Jupp.

'You removed an AIP tag?' said Boosky. 'That's impossible.'

'Not as impossible as the idea that you would escape the Bucket, go into cutspace and find yourself in the exact same place as Stanley,' said Jupp.

Boosky shrugged. 'Yeah, pretty lucky, eh?'

'Unbelievably lucky,' said Jupp. 'Which is why I don't believe you. Why are you here?'

'It's just a happy coincidence, OK?'

'A happy trillion-to-one coincidence. You followed us here so you could lead the police to Stanley and collect the reward.'

'Followed you? No way. I wouldn't help those apes and give up my old pal Stanley.'

'Watch who you're calling an ape,' said the Yeren brother threateningly. 'Many of my brothers are members of the police, and not of their own choosing.'

'I mean ape like AIP, you know. Some of my best friends are Yeren. I love you guys. You're like big teddy bears.'

The Yeren snarled at Boosky and grabbed him by the neck, lifting him so that his legs thrashed wildly in the air.

'I bet he's a snitch,' said Jupp.

'Officer Grogun did say he helped them out some-times,' said Stanley.

'Grogun?' said the Yeren.

'You know Grogey?' said Boosky, still trying to peel the hairy hands away from his neck. 'Why didn't you say? Me and him go way back.'

The Yeren growled. 'Grogun is a misguided fool like the rest of them.'

'You took the words right out of my mouth . . . ouch.' The Yeren squeezed harder.

'Are you Curlip?' asked Stanley.

The Yeren turned to look at him, loosening his grip slightly on Boosky. 'He mentioned me, did he?'

'Only that you were his cousin and that you ran off to join the League.'

'And did he tell you why so many of my kind work for the police in the first place?'

'He said your planet was in debt.'

'That's right. When the Armorians came to our planet they brought food and medicines, which they gave to us freely to begin with, then sold on credit, so we didn't have to pay immediately. Eventually we amassed a debt so large that we had nothing to pay it off with except our own labour. Armoria tricked us and effectively enslaved the entire population.'

'The same has happened on many planets,' said General P'Tang.

'Meanwhile Armoria continues to sell things to Yerendel and with high interest rates they ensure that my people will continue to be born into slavery for many generations.' Curlip tightened his grip on Boosky.

'I'm right with you,' said Boosky. 'Armoria stinks. Down with Armoria.'

Curlip lifted Boosky so that he was eye level with him.

'And now we have a spy who works for our enemy.'

'Throw him into space, Brother Curlip,' said General P'Tang. 'He deserves no mercy.'

'No, please . . . You can't rescue me then throw me into space again. Just think of all the wasted battery power bringing me here.'

'Unlike you, the battery will recharge,' snarled Curlip.

'Stanley, please . . .' yelped Boosky.

'Can't we just lock him up somewhere?' said Stanley.

'Yes, that's it, lock me up,' said Boosky desperately.

General P'Tang shook his head. 'No, we haven't enough room. Brother Curlip, put him in the airlock and prepare to eject him.'

Curlip carried Boosky to a door, which slid open. He shoved him inside and closed it.

Boosky frantically banged on the window, but the airlock must have been soundproofed because his banging and shouting made no noise.

'But, General, you can't just kill him,' protested Stanley.

'Why ever not, Brother Bound?'

'Because killing people is wrong.'

'As you know yourself, sometimes a small sacrifice must be made for the greater good. Just as you brought glory to our cause by killing President Vorlugenar, so shall we throw out this spy. Open the airlock on my count. Three . . . two . . .'

'Listen to me, I didn't kill –' A beeping interrupted him.

'What is it now?' barked General P'Tang.

'Incoming communication,' said the lemon–skinned officer.

'Hi there, man. This is Quil Tisket of Therapia. How you doing?'

On screen appeared a man with a smiling bearded face and a hairstyle that suggested he had just been enjoying a week's holiday of rolling backwards through hedges.

'Ah, Brother Tisket, good to see you.'

'You too, man. Happy felicitations. Welcome back to Therapia. I was just getting in touch to say you've got clearance to enter the atmosphere and to remind you that you're now in Therapian space, where killing is considered the most invidious of all crimes.'

General P'Tang looked at the airlock. 'But we suspect this rascal of being a spy for the AIP.'

'We all got our faults, Endal. But try not to let murder be one of them. Now, come on, get down here. I got some cloud tea brewing.'

The picture vanished. 'Shall we open the airlock?' asked Curlip.

'No, but leave him there. At least on that side of the door he won't be able to cause any harm.'

'That's all very well, General,' said Curlip, peering through the window of the door, 'except he's already gone.'

'Come on, let's go drink some cloud tea. Then maybe we can have a little boogie before we kick back and look at the sky'

As the Goodship *Gusto* entered Therapia's atmosphere, Stanley thought back to Ms Foster's English lesson about memorable experiences.

He had never been in a plane or helicopter, or canoeing or horse riding, but how many of his class had been in a spaceship as it flew down on to an alien planet? How many had witnessed the sky turn from star-speckled black to fire red as the ship entered the atmosphere and flames licked the outside? How many had felt the tranquillity of space travel give way to the violent vibration of the high-altitude winds? Or seen the flames outside burn away to reveal a deep blue sky?

'Welcome to the greenest planet in the universe,' said General P'Tang.

The ship tilted down and Stanley saw an endless land of rolling green hills.

'It's amazing, but where does everyone live?' he said.

As the ship grew nearer Stanley could see that the green land was divided by interconnecting rivers running like veins through the landscape, but he couldn't see any towns or cities.

'Each resident has a house constructed on top of a hill,' replied General P'Tang.

'I can't see any of them.'

'Their architecture is designed to blend perfectly with the natural environment.'

The ship flew lower over the landscape and Stanley noticed that each hill had a large house on top, built out of rock, with moss, grass and even trees growing over the top.

'Therapians are the most advanced race in the universe. They have given up city life in exchange for more spacious living,' said General P'Tang.

Brother Curlip entered the bridge and saluted General P'Tang. 'We've searched the ship, General, but we can't locate the thief.'

'He's a slippery character, this Boosky Retch,' said the general.

'Do you think he'll be able to tell the AIP where we are?' asked Stanley.

'Even if he does, it won't matter. They can't touch you while you're in Therapian space. We'll just have to be extra cautious when we leave. Once we land, we'll search the ship properly until we find him.'

The ship came to standstill on a level patch of grass on top of one of the hills. In front of it was a house, with moss growing liberally over the sloping walls, giving the impression that the house, with all its windows and doors, had been carved out of the hill itself.

'This is Quil's place,' said Jupp. 'What do you think?'

'It's not how I imagined the most advanced planet in the universe,' replied Stanley.

'You should have seen it before the makeover,' said General P'Tang.

'The makeover?'

'Yes, it used to be awful.'

The general gave the order to open the door. He told the rest of the crew to stay on board to make necessary repairs while Jupp and Stanley accompanied him. The large glass front of the ship lifted up and a ramp was lowered. Stanley and Jupp followed the general out. The air outside felt fresh and clean. It felt good as Stanley breathed it into his lungs.

A door in the front of the house swung open and Quil Tisket stepped out. Seeing General P'Tang he threw his arms out wide and embraced him.

'Good to see you, Endal. It's been too long. Too long, man. And this has got to be the Juppster. Look at you, lady, you're all grown up.'

Jupp smiled shyly. 'It's good to see you, Quil.'

'And you must be the one everyone's prattling about, Stanley Bound. I saw you on the news the other day, man. I don't normally watch it because it's so totally spurious, but I saw you on it. How you doing? Welcome to Therapia. Welcome to my pad. Come in. Come on, let's go drink some cloud tea. Then maybe we can have a little boogie before we kick back and look at the sky.'

'We missed the clouds'

The inside of Quil Tisket's house had high stone ceilings and was luxuriously decorated with colourful tapestries on the walls, thick rugs underfoot and large soft cushions everywhere. Considering General P'Tang had described Therapia as the most advanced planet in the universe, Stanley was surprised to see a spiral staircase, wooden window frames and doors which swung rather than slid open. It wasn't completely devoid of technology though. Each room lit up as they stepped inside and, as they entered the large kitchen, a teapot that appeared to have been carved out of a giant nut floated over from the stove and came to rest on a dark wood table.

'Cloud tea's up,' said Quil. He poured steaming hot liquid from the teapot into four mugs and handed them round.

'Thank you,' said Jupp and Stanley.

'Ah, that's good stuff,' said General P'Tang, taking a sip. 'You make the best cloud tea in the universe, Quil.'

'Thanks, man. Glad to be sharing it with you again.'

Stanley tasted the tea. It was sweet and spicy and it produced a pleasant tickling sensation as it slipped down his throat.

'You like my pad, Stanley?'

'It's great,' he replied.

'I see the planet's finished now,' said General P'Tang.

'Yeah. One or two final touches but we're basically there.'

'What was it like before?' asked Stanley.

'It was utterly spurious, man. Totally built up. We'd ripped the karma right out of everything.'

'What do you mean?'

'Look, I'll show you.' Quil waved a hand and a hologram appeared in the centre of the table. It showed a planet as seen from space, but unlike the Therapia Stanley had seen from the Goodship *Gusto*, this planet looked more grey than green.

'This is Therapia before the makeover,' said Quil.

The holographic picture zoomed in on the planet and Stanley saw that, instead of green fields, the planet was covered in enormous skyscrapers, like great forests of concrete and glass. Spaceships of every shape and size whizzed above, between and even below them, because the skyscrapers didn't start from the ground. Instead they stood on massive stilts.

'We Therapians always loved a good view,' said Quil. 'So when we started building houses, we wanted to be high enough to see above the one next door. Then the next building would come along and we'd keep building higher to see more than our neighbours, but all we did was ruin the view we had before we started.'

'This is how Armoria looks now,' said Jupp.

'That's right,' said Quil. 'We gave the Armorians a lot of ideas. The difference was that Armorians never cared much for the nature they built over, whereas we always liked our gardens.'

Stanley noticed that most of the high buildings had roof gardens, complete with lawns, flowerbeds, bushes and trees.

Quil pointed down to one of these. 'This is actual footage. You look carefully and you can see my father watering his begonias.'

Stanley leaned in to see better, but suddenly jumped back when a large flat spaceship came into view. The hologram passed through him harmlessly, causing Jupp to giggle.

'What is that?' he asked.

'That's a cloud ship,' said Quil. 'This is how bad things got. As I say, we liked our plants so we still needed rain, but no one liked the way that the rain was so unevenly distributed. Some parts of the planet got bucketloads, other places hardly any. It's the same on most planets. And you know that feeling when you get caught in the rain without your umbrella? Everyone hated that. So we decided to automate the rain.'

'Automate it?'

'Right. You know how rain works, yeah? Evaporation, condensation and precipitation? It evaporates from the ocean, then condenses into clouds and rains back down again.' Quil laughed. 'Pretty magical, man. But we Therapians, in our wisdom, decided that we could do all that ourselves. So we got rid of the oceans, installed a worldwide drainage system to collect the water and designed these cloud ships. Watch.'

Rain suddenly fell down from the cloud ship on to the city below.

'That's fantastic.'

'Yeah, kind of. I mean, they were able to distribute it evenly and, since the cloud ships operated according to a schedule, no one ever had an excuse for not having their umbrella.'

'So what went wrong?' asked Stanley, assuming that it must have led to some great disaster.

'Nothing went wrong, man. It worked just fine. In fact, Armoria uses the same system now. It appealed to their sense of control. Those cats love to control things, even themselves. Look at the Planner, man.'

'From what I've heard, the Armorians have gone further and added all sorts of nutrients, flavours and colouring to the rain,' said General P'Tang. 'I spoke to someone who had been caught in a cherryade shower.'

'But if it all worked fine, why did you get rid of them?' asked Stanley.

'Simple, really. We missed the clouds. And we missed the fields. We realised that we had spent so much time building up that we'd gotten away from what we really liked.' Quil waved a hand over the table and the picture disappeared.

'So you knocked everything down and started again?' asked Stanley.

'Yeah. We'd started to spread out on to other planets by that point and so we had enough room to redesign the place as we liked it. In fact, if anything it's even better than before because it's properly designed now. We made all these hills so we could keep our views, only now they're views of nature.' Quil stood up and walked to a window, which looked out over rolling hills.

'So none of this is real?'

'Define real, man. These are real hills, real trees, real rivers, real clouds, man. Just because your garden is designed is it any less real? Therapia is a garden, man. It's the biggest garden in the universe. You wanna hear some music now?'

Stanley had never heard anything like the music that started to play when Quil waved his hand over another part of the table. It began with an apparently rhythmless series of hoots, which were then joined by drumming, that grew louder and louder, but seemed to have no connection to the hoots. The hoots turned to howls and the drumming got faster.

Quil appeared to have fallen into a trance. His eyes were shut tight, his head swayed back and forth and his hands kept the beat on the table.

Jupp leaned forward and whispered in Stanley's ear. 'If you think the music's weird, wait until you see him dance.'

A new instrument joined in that could be best described as the sound of a wild animal eating a piano while the entire brass section of an orchestra were repeatedly thrown off a cliff.

Still with his eyes shut, Quil sprang up off his chair and started throwing himself around the room in a series of random jerky movements that made it look like he was experiencing some kind of fit.

General P'Tang remained stony-faced, but Jupp laughed and grabbed Stanley's sleeve. 'Come on,' she said. 'Let's join in.'

Stanley stood up and, a little embarrassed, started to copy Quil's movements. Oddly enough as he did so he felt like he began to understand the music. Nothing in it had changed, but it was as if it found form inside his head when he moved.

Quil opened his eyes and smiled. 'Yeah, man, lose yourself in the crazy beat.'

They continued dancing until the final note, when

all three of them collapsed on the floor laughing. It felt like years since Stanley had laughed like this. As he wiped away the tears from his eyes he felt relaxed and happy.

'Quil, we have much to talk about,' said General P'Tang seriously.

'Yeah, man. Let me show you where you'll be staying, then we'll get talking business.'

'Now, do you mind if I take a look at this wonderful talking mushroom of yours?'

Instead of his having to climb the staircase, when Stanley put his foot on the first step the whole thing spun round, lifting him to the next floor, where Quil showed him his room. It was big and airy with large windows overlooking the rolling hills of Therapia. Below his window was the flat patch of grass where the Goodship *Gusto* had landed.

'Settle yourself in. You can gather your thoughts here and come down when you feel like it,' Quil said. 'The glass is molecular, so if you want some fresh air, press this button.' He did so and the glass disappeared.

'Brilliant. Thanks,' said Stanley.

Quil pressed the button again and the glass reformed. 'You just chill out here until you want to come down.'

'Don't be too long. We have important business to discuss,' said General P'Tang.

'Oh, don't be so uptight, Endal. Now, Juppster, your room is across the hall.'

Stanley could tell that Quil's relaxed attitude was grating on General P'Tang's sense of urgency, but he felt glad to be able to shut the door on them, sit down on the large comfortable bed and have a moment to himself.

'Me hungry,' said Spore, climbing out of his pocket on to the bed.

'Hi, Spore.' Stanley found a plate of cookies and placed them on the bed for Spore to help himself.

'Me like it here,' he said, with his mouth full of half-chewed cookie. 'Me like the music noise, but me feel funny when Stanley jump around to them.'

'Sorry, I forgot you were there.'

'Me not mind. Me just happy to be with Stanley.'

'I'm happy you're here too. We're both a long way from home, aren't we?'

'What is home?'

'Home is where you come from. It's where your family are.'

'Spore's family never understand this spore.'

'I know how you feel.' Stanley picked up a cookie from the plate and took a bite. It tasted good.

'Me like the man called Quil, but not trust general man with shiny eyes.'

'General P'Tang? He's just wearing sunglasses. Why don't you trust him?'

'Because he say all everyone is the same, all everyone equal, all everyone brothers, but he not the same, he not equal, he not brother. He General.'

'That's because he's in charge.'

'In charge to lead others to fighting? Spore not like fighting. Spore used to fight with other spore over food. Fighting hurt.'

'This is different. The Armorians have done terrible things. General P'Tang wants to fight to stop them.'

'So fighting can be good thing?' Spore looked at him quizzically.

Stanley didn't know how to respond, but whatever he would have said went out of his head when another voice spoke from the doorway. 'What a remarkable life form!'

Stanley and Spore looked up to see a wild-haired man with a huge head, massively out of proportion to the rest of his body.

'I'm sorry, this isn't my room,' he said. 'You'd think with my brain capacity being three times the size of most sentient beings, that I'd at least be able to tell one door from another. But, alas, door recognition seems beyond my cognitive capability. I'd like to say that it's because my mind is focused on higher things, but the truth is I'm just not good with doors. Pleased to meet you, young man.'

'You're Professor NomVeber,' said Stanley.

'I am indeed. Of that I am almost entirely positive. One can never be fully sure of anything, of course, but I do think that there is considerable evidence to that effect. Now, do you mind if I take a look at this wonderful talking mushroom of yours?'

The professor pulled out a magnifying glass and stepped closer.

'Me Spore, not mushroom,' said Spore.

'Yes, yes, fascinating,' continued the professor, bending low to get a better look. 'It appears to be a fungus of the species *Gomphus mobilus*, commonly found in and amongst refuse.'

Spore was looking anxiously up at the magnifying glass. 'Me not like the make-things-bigger glass.'

'It's OK, Spore,' said Stanley. 'Professor NomVeber won't hurt you. He's the cleverest man in the universe. He discovered cutspace.'

The professor turned to address Stanley. 'Not strictly correct. Steppers have been using it for centuries. I simply developed the cutspace drive, which enabled the rest of us to use it. Do I know you?'

'I'm Stanley Bound. You answered my question about cutspace on the information thing.'

'I do a lot of that. I should never have agreed to it. Weren't you under arrest?'

'Yes, but General P'Tang teleported me aboard their

ship, then brought me here. What about you? Why are you here?'

'I'm here as a guest of Quil Tisket. I like Therapia a great deal, partly because that blinking Vik Noddle can't reach me here. And they've done a marvellous job on the planet. Quil's a lovely man, but I can't say I like that terrible music of his. I'm a big fan of silence myself. I have some wonderful albums of it. Now please tell me, where did you find this wonderful specimen?'

'He found me really.'

'Spore Stanley's friend,' said Spore.

'How very impressive. It's able to make personal distinctions of taste and even to form emotional attachments and communicate them. Where are you from, Master Spore?'

Together, Stanley and Spore explained how he had grown in a rubbish container, then climbed out to look for his brother and found that he was suddenly more advanced than the rest of his family.

'And none of your relatives have these abilities?' asked Professor NomVeber.

'This spore the only speaking spore,' said Spore.

'Intriguing, isn't it? The only speaking spore, and not just basic communication but a whole range of tenses, syntactic invention and emotional complexity. I'd love the opportunity to study him. I only have a few bits with me, but I should be able to conduct some rudimentary tests.'

'What kind of tests?' said Stanley.

'Only very basic ones. Nothing that would cause our little friend any distress or harm. You have my word.'

'Me stay with Stanley,' said Spore.

'Don't you want to find out why you're like you are?' asked Stanley.

'Why this spore Spore?'

'Exactly,' said Professor NomVeber. 'It won't take long. You'll be back with your friend in a couple of hours.'

Spore looked up at Stanley, then at Professor NomVeber. 'OK, I go with the big-headed one to find out why.'

'You said, I,' said Stanley.

'This is wrong?'

'No, it's right. You said I instead of me.'

'I a fast learner, yes?' said Spore.

'Exactly. And hopefully we're going to find out why,' said Professor NomVeber.

'I'm not going to start judging you just because you killed a man I liked'

As Stanley stepped on to the spiral staircase it twisted the other way and took him back downstairs. He found Jupp standing in the hallway, listening at a door. From behind the door came the sound of raised voices.

'Dad and Quil are arguing,' she whispered.

'Listen, Endal, we started the League to challenge Armoria's ideas, not to fight their police force,' Quil was saying. 'Let your words be your weapons, man. Let your words be your weapons.'

'It's all very well for you, Quil, living here, outside of Armorian control, while the rest of the universe suffers. The time to strike is now.' General P'Tang sounded angry.

'Last time they argued like this it ended with Dad setting up the Brotherhood. We didn't come back here for five years,' whispered Jupp. 'I don't want that to happen again. Quil needs to see sense.'

She tugged Stanley's sleeve and they entered the room.

'Jupp, Stanley, welcome to my rainbow room. Grab some pillow space,' said Quil, hardly sounding like a man in the middle of an argument. The room was full of colourful cushions. Quil was sprawled over several of them, while General P'Tang looked considerably less relaxed, pacing back and forth. There was no need to ask why it was called the rainbow room. Several miniature rainbows had sprung up near Quil as he spoke but as they approached General P'Tang the vivid colours became faded and muddy.

'What's making them?' asked Stanley.

'They're mood-sensitive refractions, man. They're created by positive thinking. Watch.' A rainbow shot up from near Quil and came down in front of Stanley. 'I'm thinking about the whole universe living in peace. You dig?'

'That's brilliant,' said Stanley.

'Yeah, I thought it would be a good place for this discussion.'

'It's very pretty, Quil, but we have serious business,' growled General P'Tang, causing the rainbow to vanish altogether.

'There's always time for positivity,' said Quil, sending another in his direction.

'Perhaps you can talk some sense into him, Stanley,' said General P'Tang, flapping his arms in frustration. 'Stanley knows the meaning of action. He has dealt the first blow against Armoria, bravely putting his own life at risk in order to take the life of the president.'

'Er . . .'

'Vorlugenar wasn't such a bad cookie, man,' said Quil.

As he spoke a rainbow appeared, but it didn't get far before General P'Tang replied, 'What are you talking about? Of course he was bad. He may have made a few concessions, but he was still ultimately the one responsible for everything. There's no such thing as a good Armorian president.'

'I shared some cloud tea with him a few times, you know. He wasn't a bad man.'

'You met with Vorlugenar?' said General P'Tang disdainfully.

'I was trying to make him see our point of view. That's what the League is about. It's for planets to get together and stand up for their rights. I told him that I thought Armoria had become, you know, a little heavy-handed, and that maybe it was time to peel back this whole universe-domination trip they were on.'

General P'Tang laughed. 'Hah. All these people understand is violence.'

'I don't think so, man. I think he was starting to get it.'

'This is typical of you, Quil. You see the good in everyone,' said General P'Tang.

'Is that a bad thing?'

'Yes, because you fail to see the truth.'

'I don't understand,' said Stanley. 'If you liked the president so much, why have you been so nice to me?'

'Hey, man, I take people as I find them. I'm not going to start judging you just because you killed a man I liked. We've all got our own path to stroll along.'

'Stanley did a great thing when he killed the president,' said General P'Tang. 'There is such a thing as justified killing. Armoria declared war on the universe when it decided to police it. Stanley's act was an act of war.'

'You say that like it's a good thing,' said Quil.

'I think history will show it to be not only good but a brave and important thing.'

'And clever,' added Jupp.

'Tell Quil why you did it,' urged General P'Tang.

'Yes, tell him,' said Jupp.

'I didn't do it,' Stanley said quietly.

Quil, Jupp and General P'Tang all stared at him. None of them spoke.

'I . . .' Stanley began. He wondered how it had suddenly become so difficult to tell the truth. 'They arrested the wrong person. I've never killed anyone.'

'But it was you in the footage,' said General P'Tang.

'I've seen it too, man,' said Quil. 'It sure as cosmic chutney looked like you.'

'And you said you did it,' said Jupp. 'You told me you did.'

'I lied.'

Stanley looked at Jupp and saw his own face reflected in her mirrored glasses. All the rainbows had gone from the room now.

'It's a big universe and you're going to get a lot of people telling you a lot of different things, but bear this in mind: I've got no ulterior motive'

'Jupp, let me explain,' cried Stanley, but she ran out of the room.

'I think you should explain to us too, Brother Bound,' said General P'Tang.

Stanley ignored him and ran after Jupp, taking the stairs of the spinning staircase two at a time. At the top he saw her door slam shut. He felt terrible. He wished he had told the truth from the start, but if he had done that, he wondered, would she ever have liked him at all?

'Incoming message for Stanley Bound.'

Stanley followed the voice, which was coming from his room.

'Hello?' he said, unsure where it was coming from.

'Recipient located. Putting call through,' said the voice.

A hologram of Dram Gurdling appeared. His eyes were a vivid shade of yellow.

'Dram, you're all right. How did you escape the picaroons?'

Dram's eyes whitened. 'When you've been knocking around space as long as me, you have a few tricks up your sleeve to get you out of situations like that. But it ain't me I'm worried about.'

'How did you find me here?'

'Never mind that. Kevolo knows your location.'

'Apparently he can't touch me here. We're out of Armorian jurisdiction.'

'I wouldn't bank on that. Kevolo's pretty narked about you jumping bail. You need to get on a ship and hand yourself in before you get rearrested and dragged back to the Bucket.'

'Why would I do that?'

'Because otherwise you'll be charged with jumping bail, removing a tag and attempting to pervert justice by leaving Armorian jurisdiction. Remember, I used to be a cop and I can tell you, even if it wasn't for the president's murder, this is enough to put you away for the rest of your life, no questions asked. If you turn yourself in, you can claim that you were kidnapped and taken against your will.'

'You want me to go back so I can be thrown in a tiny cell that doesn't even have a proper toilet, tried for a crime I didn't commit and defended by a lawyer who doesn't believe I'm innocent. Funnily enough, that's not the most appealing offer I've ever had.'

Dram's eyes reddened. 'It's the best offer you'll get today, kid.'

'No. I'll stay with the Brotherhood. They don't get caught,' argued Stanley.

'That's because no one's trying to catch the Brotherhood.'

'What do you mean?'

'For all their big talk, P'Tang's band of merry souls have never done anything wrong. Kevolo keeps an eye on their activities, of course, but so far they've never broken a law. Or at least they hadn't until they helped you out. You'll be putting them in as much danger as you're in if you stay with them.'

'Then I'll stay here on Therapia with Quil.'

'Hah!' Dram snorted. 'You're not the first criminal on the run to have that idea. Therapians may seem pretty laid back now, but they have the toughest immigration policies in the galaxy. You don't build an artificial paradise like this by letting any old alien crook in. Besides, they only retain their independence from Armoria because they refuse to harbour illegals.'

'I don't care what you say, I'm not handing myself in. I'd rather take my chances on my own.' Stanley turned to leave the room.

'Listen, kid. It's a big universe out there and you're going to get lots of people telling you lots of different things, but bear this in mind: I have no ulterior motive.'

'Everyone's got ulterior motives.' Stanley slammed the door on Dram's hologram.

'I have absolutely no idea. Isn't that marvellous?'

Stanley knocked on Jupp's door but there was no reply. He called out her name. 'Jupp . . . please.' He wanted to explain to her why he had lied, but what would he say? That he enjoyed the way she looked at him when she thought he was a hero?

He stepped back from the door.

'Ah, Stanley, just the man, just the man indeed.' Professor NomVeber's large head poked round the side of a door frame. 'What a remarkable mystery our little friend is. Come on in, please. Come in.' He beckoned Stanley inside.

Professor NomVeber's room was filled with bubbling test tubes, beeping machines, huge microscopes and other pieces of technology and machinery that Stanley didn't recognise.

'I thought you said you only had a few bits with you,' said Stanley.

'That's right, just the basics,' said the professor.

'Hello, Stanley,' said Spore, who was standing apparently happily in a dish of bubbling water.

'Are you OK, Spore?'

'I OK, Stanley.' Spore smiled. 'Professor big-head says I one of a kind. He says Spore special.'

'Very special indeed. Look.' Professor NomVeber enthusiastically grabbed a pile of paper from his bed and thrust it under Stanley's nose.

'What does it mean?' Stanley couldn't understand a word of it.

Professor NomVeber grabbed the paper back off Stanley and looked closely at it. 'Sorry, I don't know how I expect you to read my scrawl. I was so excited while I was writing it, you see.' He threw the paper over his head with both hands. 'Look, I'll show you. Where's my pen?'

'In your pocket,' said Stanley.

'Ah yes.' He pulled a pen from his top pocket, clicked the end, then began to scribble away in mid-air. As he wrote, the pen left a blue trace behind it, lingering in the air. Intrigued, Stanley reached forward to touch it. 'Don't do that,' said Professor NomVeber. Stanley took his hand away and saw that some of the blue ink had rubbed off on his finger. 'You'll want to wash that. It's anti-gravitational ink. If you don't wash it now, it won't ever come off.'

Stanley went to the bathroom. By the time he got back the professor had written profuse notes across the middle of the room.

'Look, see this.' He pointed out various sketches and equations. 'I did some basic species identification, DNA codes, carbon testing, and I was able to establish that my original guess was correct. Spore is of the species *Gomphus mobilus*.' He jumped to the next bit of scribble. 'I did litmus tests for radiation and light exposure and learnt that he was born and grew up inside a space station without any exposure to natural gases or sunlight.'

'Didn't we already know this?' said Stanley.

'Did we? Did we, Stanley? Yes, I suppose we did, but can we ever really know anything?'

'I thought the question was how he's able to speak,' asked Stanley.

'Exactly. How's he able to speak? Or, to put it another way, how did his cognitive awareness manifest itself in the form of verbal communication? Actually, no. I preferred the way you put it.'

'I only speaking spore.'

Professor NomVeber clicked his fingers. 'And therein lies the key. *Gomphus mobilus*, like all fungoid species, breeds in damp dark places such as refuse rooms on space stations like the Bucket. They have even been known to adapt to their environment. For example, many rubbish rooms have airlocks which operate on timer systems, ejecting the waste into space, and certain types of fungus have developed ways of clinging on, and even sometimes hiding in anticipation of this happening. I read a very interesting article in *What Scientist?* about this very recently. However, not one of the examples cited demonstrated such an advanced level of development.'

'I a quick learner,' said Spore.

'Exactly. Or, put another way, Spore's ability to learn exceeds that of even much higher evolved beings. Spore has leaped several stages of his natural evolutionary progress. How? You may well ask.'

The professor paused.

Stanley waited. 'How?' he asked eventually.

'What?'

'What's the answer?'

'This is the wonderful thing. I have absolutely no idea. Isn't that marvellous?'

'Is it?'

'Oh yes. Do you know how long it's been since I've had absolutely no idea about something? Not a clue. Not a hypothesis. Not a theory. It's a complete mystery to me.'

'And this is your discovery?'

'Exactly. I have discovered something I don't know, but something I very much mean to find out.'

'Stanley, look, hairy-faced meanies'

Stanley left the professor and went back to Jupp's door. Again he knocked and called her name, but to no avail.

'I don't think the girl with shiny eyes is in there,' said Spore, poking his head out of Stanley's pocket.

'She is. She just doesn't want to speak to me,' he replied.

'Why she not want to speak to Stanley? I like to speak with Stanley.'

'I told her the truth — that I didn't kill the man everyone thinks I killed.'

'I not understand. She not want to speak to you for telling the truth?'

Stanley turned away from the door, certain now that Jupp wasn't going to appear. 'I think she's still upset about the lie.'

'Ah, that make sense.'

Stanley went back to his room. Spore climbed out of his pocket and on to the windowsill, where he could see the blue-jacketed Brotherhood climbing over the Goodship *Gusto*.

'What is that?' asked Spore, pressing his face against the window.

'That's the ship that brought us here.'

'We will leave on it as well, yes?'

'No, I don't think so. I think now they know the truth we'll have to find another ship to leave on.'

'We not stay here?'

'No.' Stanley couldn't imagine Quil throwing him off the planet, but he believed what Dram had said about the planet's immigration laws.

'So where we go?' asked Spore.

'I don't know,' said Stanley sadly. He thought about something Jupp had said on the *Gusto*. He remembered her saying that being on the run he wouldn't ever be able to go home. He looked out at the white fluffy clouds that filled the sky. They reminded him of when he used to sit at his bedroom window and look out at the sky and imagine he was far from home. Now that he was further than he could ever have imagined, he wished more than anything that he could go home to the poky flat above the grotty pub in south London. Life had felt pretty bad at the time, but at least no one there wanted to convict him for murder.

'Perhaps we can fly in that ship instead.'

Stanley looked up to see what Spore was talking about and saw a silver spaceship breaking through the clouds. It was smaller than the *Gusto*, and its metallic body glinted in the sunlight. The workers on the *Gusto* stopped what they were doing and watched it approach.

'There were ships like that flying around outside the Bucket,' said Stanley.

'That's not surprising, since it's an AIP shuttle.'

Stanley turned round to see that Jupp was standing behind him. From the hard edge in her voice he could tell that she was still angry with him.

'I'm sorry,' he said.

'I heard what you said outside my door. You're right, you should never have lied,' said Jupp. 'Who were you talking to, anyway?'

'Stanley talk to me. I Stanley's friend. Stanley not lie to me,' said Spore, jumping off the windowsill, bouncing on his head and landing on the bed.

Jupp bent down to inspect Spore more closely. 'Hello,' she said, her voice softening. 'What planet are you from?'

'I not from any planet. I from rubbish.'

Jupp laughed.

'So are we still friends then?' asked Stanley.

The smiled dropped from Jupp's face. 'Friends? No, I'm not your friend. You betrayed my trust and put the Brotherhood in danger.'

'Well, I didn't ask to be teleported on board the ship,' said Stanley.

'Oh, I see. You'd rather have taken your chances with the Marauding Picaroons, would you?' shouted Jupp.

'At least they're not all talk, like your dad,' yelled Stanley.

'What's that supposed to mean?'

'Why you two speak so loudly?' asked Spore.

Stanley ignored him. 'It means that for all your dad's big talk, his precious Brotherhood has never actually done anything.'

'My dad is a great man. He's biding his time, that's all.'

'Hah. Your dad is scared of Armoria. He just talks tough to impress all those people he's got working for him while he pretends that everything is fair and equal.'

'Stanley, you must look,' said Spore, who had bounced back over to the windowsill.

'Not now, Spore,' said Stanley.

'My father will lead the Brotherhood in battle against the Armorians, and I'll be by his side when he does and we will liberate the universe.'

'But, Stanley, look, hairy-faced meanies,' said Spore.

Stanley and Jupp turned to see that outside the window the shiny ship had now landed just in front of the *Gusto*. The back had opened and down the ramp marched two orderly lines of Yeren AIP Officers.

'They've come for me,' said Stanley.

'But they can't arrest you outside of their jurisdiction. They have no power here.'

The guards were standing in two lines with guns at the ready, surveying the area for any potential danger. In between the two lines came more hairy-faced officers and one short fat man in a smart uniform.

'Something tells me that he's not bothered about details like that,' said Stanley.

'Commander Kevolo,' said Jupp. 'You need to hide. You can't let them catch you here.'

'Why should you care?' snapped Stanley.

'Because if they find you here, it'll be Quil and us that get into trouble. Now, hide.'

'Where?'

'You can climb out my window. That's on the other side of the building. You'll be able to get on to the roof and stay hidden until they've gone. Come on.'

'The name's Hal Shorn, and you might want to hold on to your thanks'

Stanley hurriedly followed Jupp into her room.

'Why you have to joggle me around?' asked Spore.

'Stay quiet, and stay out of sight,' said Stanley, shoving him back inside his pocket.

Hearing voices coming up the stairs, Stanley pushed the door shut behind him. Jupp pressed a button to the side of the window and the glass disappeared. Stanley leaned out. It was only the first floor, but it still looked like a long way down.

Jupp ran to the door, where the voices were getting louder.

'Hurry,' she whispered. 'I can hear Kevolo.'

Stanley put a foot on the windowsill and climbed out. The wall was built on a sharp gradient and the moss and other plant life that covered it didn't feel particularly strong, but he edged out and pushed himself flat against it.

Jupp stuck her head out of the window. 'There's a ledge above you where the roof flattens out. Climb up and hide.'

She went back inside and the glass reformed. Stanley felt his heartbeat quicken with panic. The roof had looked much more climbable than it was. He could see the ledge that Jupp was talking about, but when he moved his hand to reach it his foot slipped and he slid down a couple of centimetres. Inside the room, he could hear familiar voices.

'Hey, Kevolo, man, you got no right to come barging into my pad. No right, man,' Quil Tisket was saying.

'You will address me as Commander Kevolo, and I have reason to believe that you are harbouring a dangerous criminal, which gives me the right to search your premises under section 413b of the Therapian Independence Agreement.'

'On what grounds do you believe that, man?' asked Quil.

'They brought the boy with them on their ship,' said the distinctive voice of Boosky Retch.

General P'Tang said, 'You are a wretched little creature, aren't you?'

'I like him even less when he's on our side,' said Officer Grogun.

'Section 413b of the Therapian Independence Agreement still requires you to get a warrant,' said Quil.

'You seem remarkably well informed,' Commander Kevolo said.

'I helped draft that bit of the agreement.'

'It's a shame that you're not up to date on some recent changes in the law, then.'

'Changes? What changes, man?'

'As a direct consequence of the murder of President Vorlugenar, the recent disappearance of the suspect Stanley Bound and the ongoing problem of the Marauding Picaroons, I have declared a state of emergency. This means no warrant is necessary and that you and your Gustovian cohort will not have time to hide the murderer you're harbouring.'

'That's completely out of order. I do not recognise your authority,' said General P'Tang.

'Yeah, it's totally spurious, man,' said Quil. 'You still got to say why you're searching my pad, man.'

'I'm searching your pad, man, as you put it, because of your known links with the disruptive organisation known as the League,' said Commander Kevolo.

'The League is a legitimate protest group, man. We're just holding up a mirror to you guys.'

'We've tolerated your little protests, Quil, but now you have taken to hiding criminals the League will be outlawed. You will be forced to disband the group or else be treated as common criminals yourselves.'

'You have no right to do this,' said General P'Tang.

'And that goes for your pathetic Brotherhood too . . . Yes, I know all about you. And now I have a witness that you helped Stanley Bound jump bail.'

'You call this snivelling crook a witness?'

'Watch who you're calling snivelling,' said Boosky.

'Shut up, Boosky,' said Grogun.

'Enough of this. Senior Officer Grogun, conduct a full search for the criminal Stanley Bound.'

Stanley considered sliding down the wall but, looking down, he could see that directly beneath him an AIP officer was now standing with his back to the wall. He reached a hand up, but as he did so put too much pressure on his foot and managed to dislodge a tuft of moss which rolled down the sloping wall, landing on the guard's head. Thankfully, the tuft was small enough to land on the Yeren's thick head of hair without attracting his attention.

Stanley had to get away from the window. Any second now, Grogun would open it and find him. Stanley stretched up again, trying to reach the part of the roof where it flattened at the top, but the small shrub he grabbed had thin roots and came away in his hand. Not wanting to let go of it in case it attracted the attention of the guard below meant Stanley was now hanging on with only one hand. He lost his grip and had begun to slide down the wall when he felt a hand grab his wrist. He looked up. The hand belonged to a teenage boy with dirty blond hair and cold grey eyes. He wore colourful ragged clothes and Stanley recognised him as the one who had held a volt-dagger to his throat on the *Purple Turtle*. The boy held a finger to his lips to motion that Stanley should stay quiet, then pulled him up on to the flat roof of the building.

'Thank you,' said Stanley.

'The name's Hal Shorn, and you might want to hold on to your thanks,' said the boy.

Before Stanley could ask what he meant by this, Hal pulled from his belt a set of metal handcuffs with a long chain linking them. He slapped them over Stanley's wrists.

'What are you doing?'

Hal spun round and, using the chain, forced Stanley on to his back. 'Hold on tight and don't throw up on me,' he said.

He stretched out his right arm with his open palm facing upwards, then brought his other hand down on to it, making a loud clap. Stanley heard a tearing sound and a black hole appeared in front of them as though the clap had torn a hole in the air itself. However, the sound of the clap had attracted the attention of the guard below, who sounded the alarm. Stanley heard Grogun's voice shout, 'Who's up there? We have the place surrounded. Give yourselves up.'

While Stanley was considering whether, given the circumstances, giving himself up might not be the better option, Hal stepped into the black hole.

From the sensation that his eyeballs were being chewed by a toothless cow while his face was being turned inside out, Stanley knew that he was entering cutspace. The rolling hills of Therapia had gone. In their place were swirling patterns. Without the protection of a spaceship, the nausea of cutspace was even worse, and Stanley felt like he would have been sick had he been able to locate his stomach. And then Hal clapped his hands again and a dazzling white light appeared. Stanley shut his eyes to protect them.

He felt solid ground form beneath his feet and collapsed on to it. Laughter filled his ears. He opened his eyes to see hundreds of parrot-headed creatures looming down on him, their beaks clacking in mocking, victorious laughter.

'Move out of the way, you filthy scabs,' said a throaty voice. 'Let me see our bounty.'

The picaroons squawked approvingly and moved back, allowing someone to step into view, someone who wore a black bandanna and had a crack down the side of his orange beak. It was Captain Flaid. 'Well done, Hal, lad. Well done, indeed.'

Hal handed him the chain that held Stanley's wrists.

'And greetings to you, Stanley Bound. Welcome on board the *Black Horizon*.' Captain Flaid yanked the chain so that Stanley's face smacked against the floor.

PART THREE

DI Lockett stands on the other side of the two-way mirror, looking in on Stanley. She has given him another break, but she wonders whether she needed it more than he did. She knows that breaks give him time to work on the incredible story he is telling, but she doesn't get any sense that he is making any of it up. She has interviewed more liars than she cares to remember in that little room so she knows the signs to look for, but during the telling Stanley never once looked up at the ceiling or down at the floor to get his story straight in his head. She knows that PC Ryan is right and that he is most likely a very disturbed boy who has dreamt up this story to hide the reality of whatever happened to him during his time away, but the nagging feeling that he is telling the truth will not leave her. Something in his voice when he described how he regretted having lied to Jupp makes her think that here is a boy whose life is so damaged by lies that he values honesty above all else. Then there is the earring and the strange military jacket he is wearing.

'Are you OK, ma'am?'

PC Ryan's question snaps DI Lockett out of her thoughts and she realises that she is resting her forehead against the glass. She stands up straight and turns round to find that PC Ryan has with him a grey-haired man with thick-rimmed spectacles and a rodent-like face. He is wearing a plain grey suit and carrying a briefcase.

'This is Dr McGowan. He's the child psychologist I was telling you about,' says PC Ryan.

DI Lockett shakes Dr McGowan's hand. He has a weak handshake.

'PC Ryan has briefed me on the situation,' he says. 'I read about the boy's disappearance in the papers, of course. It sounds like a most interesting case. I understand he has an extremely vivid imagination.'

'Yes, it's certainly an engaging story,' says DI Lockett.

'Perhaps it would be best if I were to speak to him alone. An environment such as this can be extremely intimidating for a child.'

'No,' says DI Lockett forcefully. 'What I mean to say is that I'd like to hear the rest of the story myself before we ask you for a professional opinion.'

'Of course,' says Dr McGowan.

'You can sit in on the rest of the telling, if you like.'

'That would be most useful, yes.'

'Would you like to know what's happened so far?'

'No, I'm sure I'll be able to fill in the blanks. After all, filling in the blanks is my job.'

'OK, come in with me then. I'll introduce you, but can I ask you not to interrupt the story? I believe it is doing him good to tell it.'

PC Ryan holds open the door and all three enter the room to hear the next part of Stanley's story.

'If I were to go worrying myself about rights and wrongs, you think I'd be in the marauding business?'

'Let's flay him.'

'Let's fry him.'

'Let's pull out his eyes and use them as marbles.'

The picaroons jeered at Stanley and prodded him with the ends of their agonisers. It felt like a nightmare. Only worse.

'If any of you lay a feather on him, you'll have me to answer to, you squalid squawkers,' snarled Captain Flaid. He waved his own agoniser in the others' faces and they recoiled.

'Who are you to say what we does or don't does?' said a red-feathered picaroon who Stanley recognised from Dram's ship.

'I am the captain of this here vessel, that's who. And while that remains the case, Mr Conur, you nefarious no-goods will do what I says.'

Many of the picaroons cheered at this and clacked their beaks approvingly. But a significant number, Stanley noticed, the red-feathered bird included, remained quiet.

'Why have you brought me here? What do you want with me?' asked Stanley.

'Why?' said Captain Flaid. 'I thought that would be obvious. Your price has gone up. You've got as much riding on your head as I have now. After all, you is the master criminal who killed the president.' He ended this speech with a mock bow.

'I'm not. I didn't. I'm innocent,' protested Stanley.

'Now, what you've done there is gone and mistook me for someone who cares.'

The picaroons laughed.

'If I were to go worrying myself about rights and wrongs, you think I'd be in the marauding business? No. You sees, marauding isn't about who's right and who's wrong. It's about loot. And right now you is worth a rather lot of loot. Now, Hal lad, take the little one with you and keeps an eye on him.'

'Why's Hal get to look after him?' said Conur, the red-feathered picaroon.

'Because he's the only one I trust. I certainly trust him more than you, Mr Conur.'

The red picaroon snarled threateningly at Captain Flaid, but Flaid held his ground and eventually Conur backed down.

'Now go about your business. That goes for all of you,' yelled Captain Flaid. 'Fire up the cutspace drive, check the weapons. We're going to the Z1 sector. And, Hal, don't let this one out of your sight. I don't want him escaping and I don't want any of them pics touching him, neither. There's a whiff of mutiny amongst these old space birds and I don't want to give them any encouragement.'

'Yes, Captain,' said Hal.

'Good lad.'

'Come on.' Hal grabbed Stanley's shoulder and led him off the bridge, holding his volt-dagger at arm's length and waving it threateningly at anyone who got too close.

'Where are you taking me?' asked Stanley.

'To the kitchen,' replied Hal.

'Why?'

'Because I'm Flaid's cook and it's dinner time, that's why.'

'But if the captain trusts you more than any of the others, why are you working in the kitchen? Shouldn't you be first mate or something?'

'Conur is first mate.'

'But he doesn't seem to trust him at all.'

'The captain believes in keeping the ones he least trusts nearest to him so he can keep an eye on them. The ship is full of pics ready to take his place, and by day the captain can fight and win against any of them.

At night he sleeps behind a locked door with a knife under his pillow so they can't get him, but he can't fight poisoned food, can he? So he needs someone he trusts in the kitchen.'

'But why does he trust you?'

'Because I owe Captain Flaid my life. Now, get in here and quit asking questions.'

Hal shoved Stanley into the kitchen.

'That's when I saw the hole. It was like a black dot floating in front of me, but somehow I knew exactly what to do'

At home, in the poky flat above the grotty pub in south London, Stanley's kitchen could get pretty dirty at times, with piles of washing-up in the sink and over-flowing bins. But that was nothing compared with the kitchen of the *Black Horizon*.

There were thick layers of grime and filth. If there were bins under the mounds of rubbish, they had long since been lost. The crockery and cutlery were a revolting browny green colour. In the corner of the room was a TV screen so grimy that the newsreader on it was barely visible. But the most disgusting thing about the kitchen was the infestation of creatures that looked like a cross between a cockroach and a rat, but were the size of a medium-sized cat. As Stanley and Hal entered the room the creatures stopped nibbling at leftovers long enough to assess that they were no real threat, before carrying on eating.

'What are they?' asked Stanley.

'Rottlebloods,' said Hal, pushing one out of the way and grabbing a steel pot.

'They're disgusting.'

'There are worse things.' Hal filled the pan with water and placed it on a counter, crushing one of the rottlebloods as he did so. It made a crunching noise as it died. The others moved away from Hal, but made no effort to hide. 'I try to keep the population down, but they're harmless and they serve their purpose.'

'What purpose?'

'They eat all the leftovers, which means there's never enough food to tempt something really big in here.' Using his knife, Hal skilfully flipped another rottle-blood up into the pot of water, which was now boiling. It screamed as it hit the water and tried to get out, but Hal slammed a lid on and it sank into the water.

'You're going to eat it?' said Stanley, revolted.

'There's not a lot of meat on them, but they add a bit of texture.'

Stanley found a stool and sat down to watch as Hal pulled ingredients from sealed jars and threw them into the pot. Stanley could feel Spore moving around in his pocket, obviously excited by the smell of the food, but when Hal chucked in a handful of mushrooms, Spore suddenly went very still.

Perhaps it was because Hal was more interested in cooking than in intimidating Stanley that he started to feel more at ease.

'I've got a question,' said Stanley. 'We came through cutspace to get here, I know, but I thought you had to have a spaceship to do that.'

'Most people do.'

'Why not you then?'

'Because I'm a stepper, ain't I?'

'A stepper? Is that the planet you're from?'

Hal was slicing a vegetable that looked like an enormous marrow. 'For a master criminal you don't know much, do you? Stepping's an ability.'

'How's it work?'

Hal shrugged. 'I let the scientists worry about the physics of it. I just do it.'

'But you must know how you do it.'

'How does anyone do anything? How do singers sing? How do dancers dance? They don't know how. They just do it. All I know about stepping is I see a hole, clap to make it big enough, then step through it.'

'Have you always been able to do it?'

'No. I made my first step a couple of years ago.' Hal put down the knife and turned to Stanley. 'We had boarded a merchant ship and were looting and pillaging when a private security force burst out on us. They're our biggest problem these days. The AIP officers don't bother us so much, and everyone else knows better than to fight back, but these private armies don't take any prisoners. So I was down in the cargo hold with a couple of other pics when we heard the captain give the order to get back to the ship. But we were trapped, see?'

'Flaid left you behind?'

'That's how marauding is,' said Hal. 'You work together because there's strength in numbers, but when things go wrong you're on your own.'

'But you must have been angry,' said Stanley.

'Maybe I was. Maybe I thought I was different. Maybe the knowledge that it was going to be him that killed me made my blood boil. Whatever I felt, that's when I saw the hole. It was like a black dot floating in front of me, but somehow I knew exactly what to do. I clapped and stepped and the next thing I knew I was stepping back on board the *Black Horizon*, watching the merchant ship get blown up.'

'What happened to the other two pics you were with?'

'They went down with the rest of the ship, I suppose. Anyway, since then I see holes everywhere I go.'

'But if you can go anywhere, why do you stay here?' Stanley couldn't see why anyone would choose to stay more than five seconds on this ship.

'Because this is my home.'

'But you can't like it here.'

There was a pause before Hal replied. 'Most people

don't trust steppers, but on the *Black Horizon* no one trusts anyone, so I'm the same as everyone else.'

'Why don't people trust steppers?'

'Because we can go anywhere in the universe. You can't lock us up. We make the best criminals. We can step in and out of banks without trouble. That's why steppers have to be registered by the Armorian government and why lots of us are employed as spies. The ones who ain't belong to a secret society and spend their time hiding their ability. But I'm not on any register, I ain't no spy and I ain't a member of no society. When you're a marauder you don't have to follow anyone else's rules but your own. You can do what you want.'

'And that includes cooking the captain's dinner? I tell you, if I could go anywhere in the universe with a clap and a step I certainly wouldn't be cooking someone else's food in a kitchen filled with horrible creatures on a ship of vicious bird-headed pirates, but maybe that's just me.'

Hal smiled. 'You know, I'm getting to like you, Stanley Bound. Which is a pity, because there's a good chance that one of those pics is going to kill you when we try to get to the captain's cabin to take him his grub.'

'Good. There's a fight on'

'Can't you leave me here?' asked Stanley, who wanted to have no more encounters with the picaroons than was absolutely necessary.

'You heard what the captain said. I'm to keep my eye on you. Now, hold this.' Hal handed Stanley a large cylindrical container with the broth inside. 'Mind you, don't let anyone near it. The captain is your best chance of getting off this ship alive. The rest of these scoundrels will kill you just for the fun of it.'

'They made their way along the corridor. It was dark, dirty and alive with humming, clunking and rattling as if the ship was going to fall apart.

Hal stopped in front of a door. 'The captain's cabin is through the crew's sleeping quarters. It can get pretty nasty in there so keep your head down, walk quickly and do what I say. Got it?'

'Got it.'

The door slid open to reveal a large hall with rows of metal bunk beds. In the middle, hundreds of picaroons were gathered around an elevated area cordoned off with rope like a boxing ring. Their excited shouts and cheers echoed around the hall.

'Good. There's a fight on. That should keep them distracted,' said Hal.

Inside the ring were two particularly big, vicious-looking picaroons, one with purple feathers, the other with green. Both were stripped down to the waist and they were fighting each other with bare fists and snapping beaks. With their tops off Stanley could see that feathers covered their bodies, although they had worn thin in places.

'Stay low and keep moving.' Hal led Stanley along the far wall, behind a line of bunk beds. Stanley kept an eye on the fight as he crossed the room. The purple picaroon had the green one pinned against the ropes. Green kicked back, sending Purple soaring over the ropes into the crowd. Green looked down and saw a bare patch of raw pink skin on his chest where Purple had torn out a fistful of feathers. Angered by this, he let out a blood-curdling scream and flew at Purple, who had climbed back into the ring. The crowd roared in excitement and waved their fists in the air.

Stanley and Hal were halfway across the hall, but Stanley was finding it difficult to take his eyes off the spectacle. With the crowd jumping up and down he lost sight of what happened next, until the green picaroon emerged with his hand raised in the air, in a gesture of victory. Inky black blood dripped from his hands and beak.

'Not far now,' said Hal.

But with the fight over, the picaroons were dispersing in all directions.

'Hey, what's that over there?' shouted one.

'It's Hal and the boy,' yelled another.

'Run,' said Hal.

Stanley did his best, but he was hindered by the heavy container he was carrying. There came a terrifying clattering crescendo of noise as the picaroons gave chase, running around, over and through the bunks. Stanley and Hal stopped running when they saw that they were surrounded.

'Get out of it, you filthy scoundrels. None of you would dare go against the captain's orders,' yelled Hal.

The red-feathered picaroon jumped off a bunk and landed in front of them. Hal stepped back.

'You want to know what I dare to do, Hal?'

'Let us pass, Conur. You know what the captain said. The boy is off limits.'

'And what about you, Hal? Is you off limits too? Me

and some of the other pics think you're getting too big for your boots, with your fancy disappearing tricks and your special privileges. You're no picaroon and you're no marauder neither. You're nothing but a cook and cabin boy.'

Hal swung his volt-dagger at Conur. 'I'll fight you any day, but not until I've taken the captain his dinner.'

'His dinner, eh? I see you got the boy carrying that for you. Let me give you a hand with that, boy.'

Hal stepped between Conur and Stanley. 'You'll back down now, Conur.'

Conur growled. 'No soft-beak's going to tell me what to do.' He went to raise his agoniser, but Hal swung his knife. Conur jumped back as the knife singed the feathers on his neck.

'You should not have done that,' snarled Conur. 'Come on, boys.' He turned his head to beckon his followers, but there was only one picaroon behind him now. A picaroon with blue and yellow feathers and a crack down the side of his orange beak.

Captain Flaid smiled. 'Mr Conur, I thought my instructions regarding this prisoner were clear.'

'You won't be captain for ever, Flaid,' replied Conur in a low, threatening whisper.

'You care to challenge me now?' said Captain Flaid, holding his ground.

Conur looked around for some support, but the

other picaroons had fallen away. He sniffed and stepped back.

'Another time then,' said Captain Flaid. 'Ah, and I see you've got my grub, Stanley Bound. Come on – you can join me in my cabin.'

'They're a rowdy dissenting bunch of reprobates, I'll grant you that, but none of them has the guts to betray me'

Captain Flaid's cabin was behind a heavy metal door at the end of the crew's quarters. Flaid opened the door using an electronic key attached to his belt. It was a lavishly decorated room, filled with all kinds of odd paraphernalia acquired from a long career in looting. Stanley stepped inside, but Flaid held Hal on the other side of the door.

'Well done, Mr Hal. You've done well today. Very well indeed,' said Flaid.

'Thank you, Captain.'

'Now, you watch out for Mr Conur. He's in need of a proper dressing-down. I smell the stench of mutiny on his breath. So you mind how you go. He'll either try to kill you or recruit you. You know which I'd prefer.'

Captain Flaid slammed the door in his face and turned to face Stanley.

'But shouldn't you protect him from them?' said Stanley.

Flaid brought his face down to Stanley's level, his beak pressing into Stanley's cheek. 'I see my boy Hal has won you over. Remember, if it wasn't for him, you wouldn't be here in the first place.'

'I know, but there are hundreds of them and they don't seem to like him any more than they like you.'

'Are you suggesting my own crew don't like me?' snarled Captain Flaid.

'They don't seem to,' replied Stanley.

Flaid laughed. 'They're a rowdy, dissenting bunch of reprobates, I'll grant you that, but none of them has the guts to betray me. Don't worry about Hal. He's survived long enough on my ship to be able to look after himself.'

Stanley couldn't explain why he cared so much about Hal, but he couldn't let it go. 'Surely if you treat him like that he'll be more likely to betray you than give up his own life.'

'Any pic that betrays me doesn't live long to brag about it. I've had my fair share of challengers before and they've all ended up the same way. Space dust. Now, take a seat.'

Flaid grabbed the pot from Stanley's hands and pushed him backwards. He staggered, stumbled and tripped over a table, landing on a large black cushion in the corner of the room. Flaid set out two silver bowls. He opened the pot of broth, poured it into the bowls and brought one over for Stanley.

'Here, eat this.'

'I'm not hungry.' Stanley didn't fancy the idea of eating the disintegrated rottleblood, but he felt Spore kick him inside his pocket. 'All right, I'll take it.'

'Good lad.' Captain Flaid sat down at the table. 'You first.'

'What?' Stanley had been planning to give his to Spore.

'I said, you try it first. You were in the kitchen when it was made. You'll have seen if any poison went in. And all this talk of mutiny has got me thinking. So you try it first.'

Stanley picked up a spoon and sniffed at the broth. It actually smelt pretty good. He tasted it. It tasted just as nice as it smelt. Hal was a good cook. Stanley lapped it up, trying not to think about the dying screams of the rottleblood, until he felt Spore kick him again. Satisfied that the food was fine, Flaid gobbled down his broth too. The thick brown liquid oozed out of the crack in the side of his beak as he greedily ate.

Stanley surreptitiously lowered a chunk of some-thing down to Spore, but as Spore disappeared back into his pocket with it, the movement must have caught Captain Flaid's eye because he looked over. 'You up to something, lad?'

'I was just wondering if there was a planet full of picaroons somewhere so I can avoid it,' said Stanley as a distraction.

Captain Flaid laughed and brought his flat palm down on the table with a loud bang. 'There was a planet once as it happens, but that's gone. Thanks for bringing it up. I love to dwell on the annihilation of my own planet and the genocidal destruction of its population. It makes me feel warm inside.'

'I'm sorry,' said Stanley. 'Was it the Armorians?'

'No, it were ourselves. We were a warring kind of world, you see. We had so many wars going on that sometimes you didn't know who you were fighting against. We spent all our time fighting or making weapons or planning our next fight. Of course, when the Armorians came along they sold us even better weapons, the problem being that once you get bigger, better weapons you get bigger, better wars. So many were dying, the population was actually going down, but that was OK because there weren't enough farmers, see, so there was less food. Then the chemical weapons made the water undrinkable. The smart pics got off the planet at that point, because it wasn't long before they made the air unbreathable and the whole planet collapsed in on itself. It ain't much more than a shell now.'

'So you were one of the ones who got away?'

'Yep. I built this ship myself and I been here ever since.'

'How many other ships are there?'

'I wouldn't know. I mean, I've destroyed a dozen or so of them over the years, but there's bound to be more out there.'

'You mean you carried on fighting your own people?'

'Fighting, looting, pillaging and marauding, that's what picaroons do. That's how we are. Now, you just relax and get some sleep.'

He pulled a lever behind him and Stanley felt braces clamp round his arms and legs. He looked down and realised that the black cushion he was sitting on was wrapping itself round him. He tried to wriggle, but felt the cushion tighten around his limbs.

'I call this my crushion.'

The crushion was now squeezing Stanley's head as well as crushing his bones.

'I'm not sure what its real name is. That's the thing about looting – so often you take things that don't have the proper instructions with them. I've figured out how it works though. The more you try to escape, the more it hurts you. I've seen it kill people who really wouldn't relax. Once you learn not to fight it becomes more comfortable than you thought possible. So just lie back and catch some sleep. You're going to need your energy to survive on this ship.'

Stanley stopped struggling and instantly the crushion settled down. Flaid was right. It was fantastically comfortable and, in spite of his circumstances, Stanley was tired. He hadn't slept since the night on the hard bench in the Bucket cell and this was infinitely preferable. He yawned and soon fell into a deep sleep.

'With a hundred billion Armorian dollars, I might just buy me a planet to retire on, somewhere to grow old in a manner as befits an old space bird like me'

'I thought I told you never to contact me, Flaid. You know how this would look – the commander of the AIP force talking to the most wanted marauder in the universe?'

'Yeah, well, I've got something you need, so I have, Jax.'

The voices drifted into Stanley's dream.

'Hold on, let me check this line is secure . . . All right. Make it quick.'

'I got a guest by the name of Stanley Bound.'

Hearing his own name, Stanley awoke. He remembered where he was. He felt the comfort of the cushion but knew that it would turn to pain if he tried to move.

'If this is one of your tricks . . .'

'It's no trick. He's sleeping in this very room.'

The voices belonged to Captain Flaid and Commander Kevolo. Kevolo's sounded like it was coming through a speaker. It lowered to an angry hiss. 'Are you out of your mind, Flaid, contacting me while he's there?'

'Don't worry. He's fast asleep. I checked before I called you. Now, how about this reward?'

'You think you can snatch a wanted criminal from our hands and then demand payment for his return?'

'The boy wasn't in your custody when we took him,' said Captain Flaid.

'My own officers were about to catch him.'

'I don't know nothing about that. I just wants my reward for being a good citizen and handing him in.'

There was a moment's pause before Commander Kevolo spoke again. 'Oh, all right. Bring him to the Bucket and you'll get your reward.'

'No, not the Bucket and I wants special rates. I wants double what you're offering.'

'Double?'

'Double or no deal. Now, how badly do you want him brought to . . . what's that word you always like to use? Oh yes, justice.'

'You're a filthy fiend, Flaid.'

'Just the way you like me. Now do we have a deal?'

'I'll need more time to get hold of that kind of money.'

'Three Armorian days and I'll meet you on the dead planet Lunkit.'

'No. That's too near Armoria. I can't be seen doing deals with marauders.'

'That's the point. Being so close to home, you'll have to be discreet, won't you? No surprises. No ambushes. If I get any hint of a double-cross I'll kill the boy and blow every ship out the starry sky and you know I have the arsenal to do it. How would that look on the midday news?'

'You're a conniving criminal, Captain Flaid.'

'Save your sound bites, Jax. Have we got ourselves a deal?'

'I'll be there with the money.'

'Music to my ears.'

'But after this, things change. Once I've given you this money, you're fair game. No more concessions. So you'd better spend the money on your retirement because my officers will come after you.'

'With a hundred billion Armorian dollars, I might just buy me a planet to retire on, somewhere to grow old in a manner as befits an old space bird like me. As usual it is a pleasure doing business with you, Jax.'

There was a click and Stanley guessed that the communication link had been terminated. He heard a rustling noise as Captain Flaid crossed the room. He pretended to sleep, not scrunching his eyes tight but making them seem gently closed and keeping his breathing regular. It was no easy task with his heart pounding away in his chest. He smelt Captain Flaid's breath as he leaned over to check on him. Flaid snorted to himself and muttered, 'Good lad. You, Stanley Bound, are going to make me a rich old bird.'

'I may look different to the others, but when I look at you I see the same as they do: a bag of loot in a blue jacket'

The next day when Stanley awoke, Captain Flaid released him from the crushion.

'Sleep well?' he asked, eyeing him closely.

'Yes, thanks,' replied Stanley, giving nothing away.

Captain Flaid opened the door to the crew's quarters. Hal was waiting outside.

'Look after our guest, Mr Hal. I have business to attend to,' said Captain Flaid.

Stanley stayed under Hal's protection for the rest of the day, most of which was spent in the kitchen, where they couldn't be bothered by the other picaroons. On the occasions when they had to venture into the main body of the ship, Hal had to spend most of his time fighting them off.

Perhaps because of this, Stanley began to think of the

kitchen as a sanctuary. Even the rottlebloods seemed less disgusting. Not cute exactly, but more like strange pets than filthy intruders. He also enjoyed Hal's company. He was easy to talk to.

'So, master criminal, how did you get past the security and kill the president?' Hal asked. He was thinly chopping some kind of round yellow vegetable.

'I didn't do it.'

'I saw the footage of the president's death on the news and it looks like you.' He gesticulated at the TV in the corner of the room.

'I know, I've seen it too.'

'But you're sure it's not?'

'Before I was arrested I'd never even left Earth. I think I'd remember flying to another galaxy and killing a president.'

'Maybe you blacked out . . . or . . . or you did it in your sleep.' Hal poured the chopped vegetable into a frying pan. 'Or perhaps you were in a trance. Or . . . what about, it is you, but it's you in the future and you went back in time so you haven't even done it yet.'

'Is that possible?'

'Time travel's tricky, but I've heard of people doing it. You have to fly through a supernova or something, which is risky enough, but there are other problems too. There was a funny story at the end of the news the other day about a guy who hated being born poor, so he went back to give his dad information to make him rich. You know, racing tips and that. His dad, though, he didn't approve of that sort of thing and didn't much like his son for doing it so as a result he decided not to have children at all. So just like that the son suddenly vanished from existence. The funny thing was that by selling his story, the dad then became incredibly rich. Not sure whether it was true, but it was a good story.'

'I don't think I would kill the president in the future. Quil Tisket said he was a good man.'

'So if you're sure it wasn't you, don't you want to find out who it was?'

'Of course I do, but how can I? Even if I wasn't trapped on this ship, I wouldn't know where to start.'

'If it was me I'd start with Vorlugenar. I mean, what do you know about this guy you're supposed to have killed?'

'Nothing, and it's a bit late now, isn't it? What with him being dead.'

'The president was the most important man in the universe. There's bound to be loads of information on him. If I knew I hadn't killed someone, I'd try to find out as much as I could about the man everyone thought I'd killed.'

'You could help me.'

Hal laughed. 'No way.'

'But you could at least help get me off the ship.'

'Sorry, I don't want to give you the wrong idea. I like you, but I'm still a marauder. This ship has been my home since I was a baby and I've got no plans to leave. Besides, you're worth fifty billion dollars. Flaid will take most of it, of course, but we'll get our cut, and he said that if I did a good job of keeping you alive I'd be getting a special bonus.'

'And you trust Captain Flaid?' Stanley considered telling Hal what he had heard the previous night, but he knew how dangerous that would be.

'There ain't much trust on this here ship, but Flaid has never done badly by me. He brought me up as his own when he could have had me thrown into one of his broths. He's been like a father to me.'

'What happened to your real father?'

'I don't know. Never knew him.'

'Would he have been a stepper too?'

'I guess so. They say it runs in families.'

'But you won't help me get off the ship?'

'Not a chance. As I say, I may look different to the others, but when I look at you I see the same as they do: a bag of loot in a blue jacket.'

'Then I'll have to find my own way to escape.'

'Escape from the *Black Horizon*? Pull that off and I'll start believing you are a master criminal.'

'You never heard the expression that curiosity killed the rottleblood?'

For the rest of the day and the following one, Stanley kept an eye out for an escape plan. He saw no reason to hide this from Hal, who, far from being concerned by his intention to escape, found it extremely funny.

Stanley's first thought was the teleport deck.

'You mean the teleport deck which is manned around the clock by at least three picaroons, all of them armed with agonisers?' Hal smirked.

'Yes,' admitted Stanley.

'The one that would require someone else to operate it while you go through?'

'You could do it,' said Stanley hopefully.

'Ha, not a chance. You keep forgetting I'm not on your side here.'

Stanley's next idea involved getting out through the

connecting tubes that the picaroons used to board other ships.

'That kind of relies on there being a ship on the other end of it, don't it?' said Hal. 'And even if we did dock with another ship, who's to say that the captain wouldn't blow it out of the sky? He normally does.'

Stanley and Hal delivered food to the captain three times a day, the final time being the evening meal when Hal left Stanley with him. By the end of his second day, Stanley was beginning to think Hal was right, there was no way of escaping the ship. Even if he had found a way off, the only time that he wasn't under constant surveillance was when he went to the toilet in a tiny room that smelt so bad that he had to hold his breath to avoid being sick.

During these moments Spore, who seemed quite at home with the stench, would climb out of Stanley's pocket to avoid any danger of falling into the cesspit of a toilet.

'I do not like it here with those beaky featherheads,' said Spore.

'I know, me neither, but I don't know how to escape,' said Stanley.

'You said this word escape before. What does it mean?'

'It means to get out of this place.'

'I see. It is the same word that the girl with the shiny eyes used when she showed you the little rooms.'

'You mean Jupp? Of course, the escape pods. This ship must have escape pods too.'

But when he put the question to Hal, he said, 'Escape pods on the *Black Horizon*? I don't think so. This ship goes down, we all go down with it.'

The next morning Stanley sat in the kitchen watching Hal wrestle a spoon from the jaws of a rottleblood, a battle which he eventually won by sending the rottleblood flying into the omelette he was making.

The news channel was on the smeary TV in the corner of the room. Mostly it had been boring reports about an economic crisis affecting the universe and record highs in unemployment, but Stanley was distracted from the chaos of Hal's cooking by hearing his own name.

'This morning Jax Kevolo, commander of the Armorian Interplanetary Police, confirmed rumours that Stanley Bound has jumped bail.'

Commander Kevolo appeared on the screen. He was standing behind a podium with journobots bobbing up and down in front of him. 'Stanley Bound has indeed broken the conditions of his bail, but rest assured, I have personally ensured that he will be rearrested soon, when he will stand trial for his terrible crime.'

'What about the rumours of you standing as president?' asked a journobot.

'Ah well . . .' Commander Kevolo smiled. 'I'm glad you asked that question. Today I can confirm that the time has come for me to give in to the numerous requests to stand for the presidency. But it is with humility and selfless intentions that I do this. Armoria needs a leader and too many of my well-respected colleagues have insisted that I stand for me to ignore these calls to action.'

There was a bustle of excited noise from the journobots, but Commander Kevolo selected the same one again to ask the next question.

'What kind of president will you be if you are elected?'

'Another excellent question.' He leaned forward on the podium. 'As you know, I was a great friend and admirer of the late President Vorlugenar. However, like many, I did occasionally find his diplomacy a little soft around the edges. Having spent some years in service of Armoria and, indeed, the universe, and having fought a constant battle against the Marauding Picaroons, I know that the strong arm of the law is required to defeat these criminals who think they are above the law. It is this tougher approach that I will bring to the presidency if I am elected.'

'And would you say that the marauding problem is now under control?' It was the same journobot again who asked the question.

'Yes, indeed. I'm pleased to say that there are fewer picaroon ships in the universe now than there were when I took the job as commander.'

Hal, who was watching now too, laughed and said, 'That's because we keep blasting them to bits.'

'And what of those who remain?' asked the same journobot.

Commander Kevolo clenched his fist. 'Those that remain will be dealt with swiftly and decisively by my officers.'

'Even the *Black Horizon*?' It was a different journobot who blurted out this question and Commander Kevolo glared angrily at it before answering. 'The *Black Horizon* is just a ship like any other, and Captain Flaid's days are numbered. Thank you. The press conference is now over.'

'He's been saying that for years, but we haven't seen even a hint of bother for ages.' Hal switched off the TV. 'Come on, let's take the captain his lunch.'

Normally the bridge of the *Black Horizon* was a fairly relaxed place. At least, relaxed compared to the rest of the ship. Under the watchful eye of Captain Flaid, sitting in his swivel chair, the crew members fought less amongst themselves than they did elsewhere. But when Stanley and Hal entered with the captain's food, there was a distinct tension in the air. Captain Flaid was on his feet, shouting at the crew.

'Will one of you mucky scabs tell me what ship I'm looking at?' he yelled.

On the large screen, a menacing-looking spaceship, armed to the hilt, loomed ominously.

'It looks like another marauding ship, Captain,' said a crew member with dirty white feathers and a brown beak.

'I can see that, you no-good featherhead.' Captain Flaid swung his agoniser at the crew member, who ducked just quickly enough to avoid serious damage. 'But what ship is it? Where's my first mate? Where's Mr Conur?'

'I'm right here, Flaid.'

Everyone on the bridge looked up to see Conur's ugly red face filling the large screen.

Stanley wondered whether it was a look of annoyance or admiration that crossed Captain Flaid's face before he spoke next. 'Explain yourself, Mr Conur.'

'Captain Conur, if you please. This here is my ship, the *Fragmented Storm*, see.' Behind him, Stanley could make out more picaroons sitting on a bridge that looked very similar to that of the *Black Horizon*.

'And there was me thinking that you had your beady greedy eyes on my ship,' said Captain Flaid.

'Oh, I do that. I do indeed. I'll be taking your crew off you in good time and your booty and, of course, your most valuable possession, the boy Stanley Bound.'

'Blast them to smithereens!' shouted Captain Flaid, with a wave of his hand.

'Ah, now that might be a problem, seeing as how I disabled your weapons before teleporting aboard,' said Conur.

'It's true, Captain,' said a crew member looking at the dials on the display.

Suddenly the *Black Horizon* shook violently and Stanley fell over, dropping the broth, which spilt out across the floor. Hal grabbed Stanley and hauled him to his feet, keeping a firm hand on his elbow.

Conur's throaty laugh reverberated around the bridge. Captain Flaid had a look of steely determination in his dark eyes.

'As you can see, the weapons on the *Fragmented Storm* are working just fine,' cackled Conur. 'And don't even think about sending that little stepper aboard to do your dirty work for you, because I'm ready for him too.'

'You're a wretched villain, Conur.'

'Just like yourself, Flaid. Half your crew are primed and ready to follow me. Take a look around you, Flaid. How much loyalty do you think you have left?'

Stanley noticed that a number of crew members had stepped away from their desks and were clutching their agonisers and looking at Flaid, although it was unclear which were looking to fight and which were ready to defend him.

'Now send the boy over and we'll negotiate your surrender.'

'And how exactly am I supposed to send the boy over when you've already used the teleport?'

'We'll be docking with you now. Send him through

the connecting tube. Once he's safely here, we can talk. And remember, I've got spies all over your ship.' Conur laughed again. 'The reign of the *Black Horizon* is over, Flaid. There's a new captain now.'

'You seem to have thought of everything, Mr Conur. I have no choice but to comply with your wishes. I'll send the boy down to the docking bay now.'

'It's nice to be so popular'

The screen that had shown Conur's face went blank and Captain Flaid spun around and grabbed the microphone he used to address the whole ship.

'Listen up, you filthy feathered fiends, because this is your captain speaking, and I don't cares if you are planning to betray me or not. The facts is like this. We are about to engage in battle and you can live or die fighting with or against me. It's up to you to decide which of these is less likely to get you killed, but it seems to me that Conur won't have half as many pics on board that ship as he's pretending so we got every chance of beating them if you sticks with me. So I want every last one of you down at the docking bay ready to fight, and should you choose to fight against me and pick the weaker side, so be it. I'll be ready to tear the feathers from your faces.'

Captain Flaid put the microphone down and turned to the crew on the bridge.

'That goes for all of you lot too, you wretched rogues,' he added. 'Get yourselves down to the docking bay. I'll join you in a minute. Today we'll dine on the bones of victory, washed down with the black blood of traitors.'

The crew cheered at this and waved their agonisers in the air as they left the bridge.

'But, Captain,' said Hal, 'how can we fight against an armed ship?'

Captain Flaid turned to face him.

'You're a good lad, Hal, but you've got a lot to learn. Conur's not stupid. He won't want to risk losing the most valuable thing on this ship.' Captain Flaid lowered his large head to Stanley's level. 'That'll be you, Stanley Bound.'

'It's nice to be so popular,' said Stanley.

Captain Flaid laughed, his beak clacking noisily, and Stanley found himself wondering whether he had detected a note of fear in the captain's mirth.

'Hal, my boy, I'm going to be busy reminding those double-crossing pics down there where their loyalties lie, so I need your help. You're the only one I trust – you knows that, don't you?'

'Yes, Captain,' said Hal.

'Good. First I needs you to deliver the boy to my

cabin. Put him in the crushion in the corner.' He handed him the electronic key from his belt. 'Then I needs you to get this ship's weapons working again, and as soon as you do, blast that *Fragmented Storm* into fragments.'

'What if you're on board the ship by then?'

'Don't you worry about me, Hal. You just do as you're told. I can't trust anyone but you. I needs to keep the rest of this crew where I can see them. If you're lucky enough to kill me, then the *Black Horizon* is yours.'

'Yes, Captain.'

'Good lad. Now off with the both of you. I've an army to lead and a battle to win.'

With Hal close behind, Stanley ran through the ship to the cabin. The corridors were even more chaotic and dangerous than usual, with heavily armed picaroons rushing down to the docking bay. Some lurched at Stanley as they saw him approach, but Hal was quick to bat them off. Most were busily engrossed in discussions about whether they should remain loyal to Captain Flaid or switch sides to fight with Conur.

When Hal and Stanley arrived at the door at the far end of the crew's quarters, Hal opened it and pushed Stanley inside. 'Where's this crushion then?' he asked.

'He means this,' said Stanley, sitting down. 'What will you do if the rest of the crew do turn against him?'

'Those renegades will follow whoever they think is

most likely to keep them alive and make them rich. Captain Flaid has fought off mutinies before. This is no different.'

'I don't suppose you're going to leave me the key, are you?' asked Stanley.

Hal laughed. 'You've got a sense of humour, I'll give you that. I'll see you around, Stanley Bound.'

'Destination Armoria'

Alone in Captain Flaid's cabin, Stanley stood up, grateful that Hal didn't know what the crushion looked like. He lifted Spore out of his pocket and placed him on Captain Flaid's desk.

'Why Hal not help Stanley? I was thinking he not like the beak people,' said Spore.

'Yeah, well, what difference does it make what he's like?' asked Stanley, sitting in Flaid's chair. 'He still follows Flaid's orders, so he's just as bad as the rest.'

'So we not able to escape after all?'

'I don't think so. Flaid's cabin is the most secure room in the ship. That's why they put me here.'

'I think Captain beak person might need escape too.'

Spore's words slowly sunk in. 'Flaid might need to escape . . .' said Stanley. 'Of course.'

'Of course what?'

'Flaid designed this ship, and I bet he gave himself a way to escape. I reckon there's an escape pod in this room that only he knows about.'

Stanley leaped up and ran to a wall. He began to check it with the palms of his hands.

'What you doing?' asked Spore.

'I'm looking for a door like the one for the escape pods on the *Gusto*.'

'I help.' Spore jumped off the desk, flying up high before turning and soaring back down, like an Olympic diver. His head hit the floor and sent him springing back into the air. He somersaulted and landed next to Stanley with a forward roll.

Stanley pushed away piles of stolen goods, expensive-looking jewellery and strange gadgets in order to get to the wall, while Spore bounced up and whacked his head against it.

DINK, went his head on the wall.

'Mind you don't hurt yourself,' said Stanley.

DINK. 'No, I OK, Stanley.'

'Doesn't that give you a headache?'

DINK.

'Have it your own way, but don't say I didn't warn you.'

DONK.

Stanley stopped what he was doing and went to where Spore had last whacked his head. He tapped

212

along the wall. *DINK . . . DINK . . . DONK*. It was a different noise. Stanley pushed away the surrounding bits and pieces and found a door handle. He turned it.

'You've found it,' he said.

Behind the door was a small padded room with a control panel and a window overlooking the endless emptiness of space.

'Welcome to the Series 64,000 escape vessel. Please take your seat and close the door to initiate disconnection from craft,' said a friendly-sounding female voice.

Spore jumped on to Stanley's shoulder. 'So we escape now?'

'Yes, come on,' said Stanley.

They climbed inside and Stanley sat down. For Captain Flaid it would have been pretty cramped, but for him and Spore there was plenty of room.

'Please close door to initiate disconnection from main vessel.' As the voice spoke one of the buttons on the control panel lit up.

'Are you ready for this?' said Stanley.

'Spore ready.'

Stanley pressed the button. The door behind them slid shut. There was a whirring noise followed by a clunk and a jolt.

'Disconnection successful. Scanning for the nearest habitable planet,' said the voice.

As the pod drifted into space, it rotated so that Stanley could see the *Black Horizon*. He was pleased to be leaving the terrifying ship. No matter where he went next, he thought, it couldn't be as bad as that. The pod continued to spin, causing the ship to disappear from sight. When it next appeared they were far enough away to see the other ship. The *Fragmented Storm* looked very similar to Flaid's ship, but Stanley could tell that the first bolt of energy came from one of the cannons on the *Black Horizon*. In the silence of space the blast made no noise, but it was clear that it had made impact. The *Fragmented Storm* sent a blast back.

'Hal must have got the weapons working,' said Stanley.

Once again the pod turned, taking the ships out of vision.

'Turn round. I can't see,' said Stanley.

'Thrusters will fire when destination has been located,' replied the computer calmly.

In its own time the pod turned full circle to show that the two ships had now separated with the connecting tube floating free. Both were now shooting at each other continually, but the amount of damage they had inflicted on each other made it no longer possible to identify which was which. Then suddenly and silently a blast from one ship split the other in half. Two more hits and the broken ship was nothing but debris floating in space.

'Which ship was destroyed?' asked Spore.

'I don't know, said Stanley.'

'Destination located. Firing thrusters,' said the computer.

'What's the destination?'

'Destination Armoria.'

'Twenty seconds to self-destruct'

Entering the atmosphere of an alien planet for the first time had been an unforgettable experience, but Stanley's second time was equally exciting. This time he was in an escape pod made of such thin material that as it entered the atmosphere he could feel its sides heat up. As it hit the high-altitude winds it was thrown about like a dinghy in a storm. Stanley and Spore laughed as they bounced off the soft walls, but Stanley was pleased when it stopped.

'Please state required destination on Armoria,' said the computer.

'I don't know,' said Stanley.

'We go see Professor big-head?' asked Spore.

'Name not recognised,' said the computer.

'Professor NomVeber. He lives here. Good idea,

Spore,' said Stanley.

'Destination selected: the residence of Professor NomVeber.'

Looking down at the surface of the planet, there was so much movement Stanley didn't immediately understand what he was looking at. It took him a minute to understand that the slowest-moving objects were the huge rectangular cloud ships. Above and below the cloud ships were countless rows of smaller moving objects. As he got closer he could see that these were various kinds of vehicles, some the size of cars, others more like articulated lorries and buses, with flying motorbikes whizzing in between.

Stanley's pod hovered over the top lane, where the traffic was moving fastest. Then the pod dropped down into it, causing some kind of flying bus behind to slam on its breaks, swerve and beep its horn. At least Stanley assumed it was its horn which sounded, because the entire sky was so full of beeping and swerving and revving engines that it was difficult to work out which sound was coming from where.

Row by row, the pod descended, past the cloud ships, to the slowest lane, which ran just above the top of the skyscrapers that covered the entire planet's surface. It reminded Stanley of what Jupp had said about the hologram of Therapia before the makeover looking like Armoria.

Even though it had been daylight when he entered

the atmosphere, this far down, below the layers of traffic buzzing overhead, it felt like dusk. In order to counter-act this, the huge buildings had bright lights on the top, shining down on the outside areas and giving those in their rooftop gardens the impression that it was a bright sunny day.

The escape pod broke from its lane and headed down towards one of the buildings.

'Landing location within range. Please prepare for landing. This vessel will self-destruct twenty seconds after landing. Please ensure you are a safe distance from the vessel to avoid injury or death,' said the computer calmly.

'What?' exclaimed Stanley. There wasn't room to move any distance away on the tiny roof garden where they were coming in to land.

'Landing location within range. Please . . .'

'Yes, yes, what was the bit about self-destructing?'

'She said the vessel will self-destruct in twenty seconds,' said Spore, clearly proud of himself for remembering this correctly. 'What is self-destruct?'

'It means that it will blow up.'

'Why it blow up?'

'I don't know.' The pod was getting close to the rooftop. 'Why are you going to blow up, computer?'

'Self-destruct setting selected.'

'It must be something Captain Flaid did so he couldn't get followed,' said Stanley. 'Computer, can I unselect it?'

'Unable to deselect self-destruct setting. Apologies for any inconvenience,' said the computer.

The pod hovered above the roof garden. Stanley could see a set of glass doors, and through the glass Professor NomVeber standing in a room full of strange apparatus and bubbling concoctions.

'Prepare for landing,' said the computer.

'Spore, climb into my pocket,' said Stanley. 'When we land we'll have to get inside the building as soon as possible.'

'OK.'

Spore climbed in as the pod landed softly on the roof.

'Landing successful. Door opening.'

The hatch popped open and Stanley rolled out.

'Twenty seconds until self-destruct.'

Stanley ran to the glass doors and banged on them. 'Professor NomVeber!' he shouted, but the professor didn't react. The doors must have been soundproofed to cut out the noise from the traffic above.

'Fifteen seconds until self-destruct. Please clear the area.'

'Professor NomVeber, please . . .' yelled Stanley.

The professor still had his back turned. It looked like he was muttering to himself, but Stanley couldn't hear him.

'Spore, what are we going to do?' said Stanley, but Spore didn't respond either. Stanley looked inside his pocket. Spore wasn't there. 'Spore?' He looked back at the pod.

'Ten seconds until self-destruct. Thank you for flying with this Series 64,000 escape vessel. We hope your experience has been a pleasant one.'

'Spore?' screamed Stanley. He must have fallen out of his pocket when they landed. But where was he now? He was about to run back to check the pod when he felt a hand land on his shoulder. He turned round.

'Stanley Bound! Well, I never. Lovely to see you,' said Professor NomVeber.

'Five seconds to self-destruct.'

'We need to get inside,' said Stanley.

He pushed Professor NomVeber back into his lab and the door slid shut just in time for them to watch the escape pod explode and bits of it bounce soundlessly against the window.

'Where's Spore?' said Stanley desperately.

'I here,' replied the small voice. 'I climb in through smaller hole to tell the professor to let us in. This good plan, yes?'

Stanley smiled. 'Yes, Spore. That good plan.'

'We have some big decisions ahead of us, decisions that will define what kind of planet we are'

'How nice of you to pop in. Everyone was most intrigued by your sudden disappearance on Therapia,' said Professor NomVeber.

The room was packed with bubbling tubes and beeping machines.

'We were taken by the beaky people but we escape,' said Spore.

'What happened to Quil and General P'Tang? Were they arrested?' asked Stanley, although he was thinking mostly of Jupp.

'Oh no, that would have incurred far too much paperwork for Commander Kevolo,' replied the professor. 'For all his big ideas of states of emergency, arresting a native Therapian and his house guests with nothing more than one unreliable eyewitness would have been an extremely lengthy process.'

'I saw on the news that he's standing for president.'

'Yes, I saw that too.' Professor NomVeber picked up a test tube and examined the contents. Replacing it, he jotted down his findings in a notepad.

'Don't you think it's a bit suspicious?' asked Stanley.

'Why would I think it was suspicious? Jax Kevolo has always wanted the president's job. Everyone knows that.'

Stanley wasn't sure whether to tell the professor what he had overheard in Captain Flaid's cabin. Since his time on board the *Black Horizon* he was beginning to wonder whether he could truly trust anyone, but it wasn't Commander Kevolo that concerned him right now. There was something else he needed to do. 'I'd like to find out more about President Vorlugenar,' he said.

'Well, you're welcome to use the information service. As a contributor, you see, I get a free subscription but it's no use to me. That's the problem with being so clever – there really is very little left to learn. That's why I was so pleased when you introduced me to your little mushroom friend here. I've been thinking a great deal about him, and there is something I can do that may help unlock the mystery. Perhaps you could leave him with me while you avail yourself of the information service.'

'Spore stay with Stanley,' said Spore.

'I have a new packet of Solar Fruit Twisties I've just opened. Are you hungry, Spore?'

'I hungry, yes.'

'There we are then. We'll be through here. Do you remember how to activate the infogram?' Stanley nodded and the professor left with Spore.

Alone in the room, Stanley said, 'I don't understand.'

A hologram of the overly tanned Vik Noddle appeared in the centre of the room. 'Hey, there. Welcome to Armorian Information Services. What can I help you with today?'

'I want to know about President Vorlugenar,' replied Stanley.

'Sure thing. Please make yourself comfortable and we'll begin.'

Stanley found a stool and sat down to watch as Vik Noddle presented him with a series of documentaries, interviews, speeches and political debates that took him through President Vorlugenar's career. He learnt that, from a young age, Vorlugenar was a charming and intelligent man, who grew up to become the most popular president in Armoria's history. He was even liked by many of the inhabitants of other planets. There was a news item about his attempt to give Armorian moon dwellers fairer rights and to increase the numbers of non-Armorians in positions of power in the AIP force.

But it was one particular interview given weeks before his death that stood out for Stanley. President Vorlugenar sat in a moodily lit studio opposite the interviewer, who had two heads, one of which nodded sympathetically every time he spoke, while the other wore a look of disbelief.

'I believe that we Armorians should question some of our core values,' said President Vorlugenar. 'Take the Planner, for example. Are we sure that evolution acceleration is a good thing?'

'Are you suggesting that the machine hailed by most as the best invention in our history is not a good thing?' exclaimed the interviewer's right head.

'No, I'm simply saying we should examine these things. Complacency is an ugly trait.'

'That's a very interesting point,' said the interviewer's left head.

'Interesting? It's borderline insane,' said the other head. 'The Planner has been helping Armorians achieve their potential for generations. It's the chief reason why our planet is the single most successful planet in the universe.'

'This is true,' said President Vorlugenar. 'The Planner has been a tremendous gift and its contribution is irrefutable, but I want us to examine any negative effects. It seems to me that it cuts down individual choice. For example, until the point you were told you were destined to become an interviewer and grew your extra head I imagine you could have done lots of other things. How did you feel about having your options limited?'

'He's got a point. At the time we wanted to be a

stratoski instructor,' said the head on the left.

'This isn't about us,' said the head on the right. 'It's about whether the president is permanently taking the Planner out of use.'

'Are you?' asked the other head.

'At this stage it has been taken out of use subject to a detailed review of its role in Armoria's future.'

'What about the AIP force? Some have suggested that you plan to reduce its size.'

'These are all matters I am considering. I believe we are at a new stage of our development. We have some big decisions ahead of us, decisions that will define what kind of planet we are. Should we be looking to increase our control in the universe, or should we have other priorities?'

'What kind of priorities?' asked the interviewer's left head.

'Perhaps there are more important things than domination and power?'

'And how does Commander Kevolo feel about the threat to his police force in view of the increase in intergalactic crime?' asked the right head.

President Vorlugenar smiled. 'Jax Kevolo and I don't always see eye to eye, but I'm sure he understands and respects my point of view.'

'Well, sadly we're out of time,' said the left head. 'President Vorlugenar, many thanks.'

The interview ended and Stanley dismissed Vik

Noddle. He wondered what it all meant. President Vorlugenar was intending to cut the size of the AIP force. Wasn't that the perfect reason for Commander Kevolo to have him killed? Also, Kevolo had always wanted Vorlugenar's job and he needed a way to get rid of him that would increase his own popularity. What better way than to have him killed and then catch the killer himself? It was perfect.

Stanley needed to talk to someone about it and decided that he would simply have to trust the professor. He went to the door where Professor NomVeber and Spore had gone and pressed the button next to it. It slid open, but it wasn't the professor who stood on the other side. It was Commander Kevolo with two AIP officers on either side and a journobot hovering behind him with a camera pointing in his direction. Stanley turned round, looking for an escape route, and saw a shiny AIP shuttle loom into view on the other side of the window. He looked back at Commander Kevolo, who was wearing a wide grin.

'Stanley Bound, you are under arrest for jumping bail, resisting re-arrest and, of course, for the murder of President Vorlugenar.'

PART FOUR

'How did they find you?' asks DI Lockett. She hadn't meant to interrupt the story, but this latest twist has taken her by surprise.

Stanley looks into her eyes. For a moment he wonders whether she actually believes him. He knows the story he is telling is pretty unbelievable but he is telling it because she asked him for the truth. Besides, it helps to put it in order in his own head. He is seeing the clues that he failed to pick up on at the time.

He certainly doesn't expect anyone to believe it. He knows that the psychologist is looking for a hidden meaning behind his story, but he decides to answer DI Lockett's question because he thinks there is a part of her that wants to believe him.

'Professor NomVeber called them,' he says.

'The professor gave you away?' she exclaims.

PC Ryan coughs, clearly embarrassed by his superior's behaviour.

DI Lockett ignores him and says, 'I thought he was one of the good guys.'

'I'm not sure I believe in good guys and bad guys any more,' says Stanley.

'Fascinating. Absolutely fascinating,' says Dr McGowan, leaning forward. 'There is certainly a moral ambiguity in many of your characters. For example, I felt that you painted quite a sympathetic picture of Captain Flaid when his men turned against him.'

'They were picaroons, not men, and I never said I felt any sympathy for him.'

'But you did appear to like the character Hal,' says Dr McGowan, consulting his notes. 'And as Captain Flaid pointed out, he was the one who kidnapped you.'

'Yes,' says Stanley.

'Sorry, I shouldn't have interrupted you,' says DI Lockett, who finds Dr McGowan's comments annoying. 'Please continue.'

'Yes, please do carry on. It's a fascinating story,' says Dr McGowan.

Stanley is unnerved by the psychologist's intense stare and the way he knits his fingers together. Stanley knows that he uses the word story because he believes it is made up, but he doesn't care. One of the things his adventure has taught him is that there are some people who won't believe anything until they are faced with indisputable evidence.

'In matters of security it is up to the commander responsible to assign a prosecutor and judge to a case, based on the most qualified person available at the time'

After his arrest, Stanley didn't see Commander Kevolo again until they were was back on board the AIP Bucket. On the shuttle ship he was put under the constant surveillance of a large group of Yeren guards, who refused to answer any of his questions so he was unable to find out what had happened to Professor NomVeber. Before being thrown into a small squalid cell, which may or may not have been the same one as before, he was thoroughly searched and his watch was confiscated. He was glad that Spore wasn't with him to be found but, sitting alone in his cell that evening, he missed his company.

On the TV in the corner of the room Stanley was headline news again. Watching the footage of his re-arrest, Stanley realised how rehearsed Commander

Kevolo's line sounded. For him it had been yet another photo opportunity.

'Once again, political analyst Lawn Waxy joins us in the studio to discuss this latest development. Lawn, what effect has this had on Commander Kevolo's chances of becoming the next president?' asked the newsreader.

'The latest figures put the commander way ahead in the polls.' A graph behind him illustrated this.

'It certainly seems that Commander Kevolo can do no wrong, but what kind of president would he be?'

'A crooked one,' mumbled Stanley at the TV.

'I think we can expect a change of approach,' said Lawn. 'Whereas President Vorlugenar was in the process of softening Armoria's approach to intergalactic policy, I think it's safe to say that Kevolo as president will be planning to assert its position of dominance in the universe.'

'In fact, he has previously suggested pushing Armorian boundaries even further beyond this galaxy, hasn't he?'

'That's right. In a speech last year he mentioned certain pre-contact planets in other galaxies that were ready for inclusion.'

'Yes. In fact, Stanley Bound is from one such planet, isn't he?'

'He is indeed – a planet called Earth that has not yet had intergalactic contact.'

The newsreader laughed. 'Talking of which, the trial

starts tomorrow. Don't miss our constant coverage on AISN, the channel that brings you the news as it happens.'

So that's it, thought Stanley glumly. He had been set up to give Commander Kevolo an excuse to subject Earth to the same treatment as Gusto and Yerendel and all those other planets that Armoria claimed to have discovered.

The cell door opened and a guard said, 'Come on, you're wanted in the commander's office.'

Commander Kevolo's office was a stark contrast to every other part of the Bucket that Stanley had seen. It was carpeted, clean and didn't smell of body odour and rotten vegetables.

Three of the four walls were covered in certificates, honours and photos of Commander Kevolo shaking hands with apparently important people. The fourth wall was transparent and revealed behind it the infinite constellations of outer space.

The commander sat behind a large desk, watching the news. He grinned at Stanley as he entered. 'Have you seen this? Your escape attempt has made me even more popular. If I didn't know better, I'd think you were on my side.' He laughed.

Before Stanley could respond the door slid open and Eddie Skulk entered, with Dram Gurdling close behind him.

'This is an outrage, Kevolo,' proclaimed Eddie.

'By that I presume you're referring to you and moonboy here barging into my office without permission?'

Dram's eyes turned a vivid scarlet colour but he let Eddie respond.

'You know perfectly well what I mean. Tomorrow you will be acting as prosecution. Therefore private consultation with the accused could be seen as an attempt to intimidate him prior to the trial.'

'Calm down, Skulk,' said Commander Kevolo.

'Intergalactic law clearly states in clause 3345 of –'

Commander Kevolo interrupted him. 'Before you start quoting the whole law book at me, you should know that prosecutor isn't my only role in tomorrow's proceedings.'

'What's that supposed to mean?'

'I'm the judge, Eddie.'

'What?' said Stanley, Dram and Eddie at once.

'That's out of order, Jax, and you know it,' said Dram.

'In matters of security it is up to the commander responsible to assign a prosecutor and judge to a case, based on the most qualified person available at the time. Guess what, boys? That's me.'

'But that contravenes Armorian guidelines to ensure a fair trial.'

'Those guidelines can be overturned in matters of security such as these.'

'What matters of security?'

'I have reason to believe that Stanley is part of a wider conspiracy against Armoria.'

'That's ridiculous. This trial will be unfair.'

'Don't worry. The verdict will still be decided by an independent cross-planetary jury.'

'You're a cheat and a liar, Jax,' snarled Dram.

'He set me up in the first place,' put in Stanley.

'I wouldn't put it past him.' Dram's eyes turned a deeper shade of burgundy.

Commander Kevolo turned to Eddie and said, 'Interesting new tactic you're going for, Eddie – accusing the prosecutor and judge. Do you mind if I quote your client and employee at tomorrow's trial?'

'Stanley, as your lawyer, I highly recommend you do not make any hasty accusations, which may damage your chances at trial. And Dram, shut up.'

'But he did it,' yelled Stanley. 'He set me up so he could become the next president. Everyone knows they didn't get on.'

'Stanley, I urge you . . . These statements will be highly damaging if repeated in court.'

'The boy's got a point though,' said Dram. A hint of blue coloured his eyes.

Eddie turned angrily to look at him. 'Dram, keep your opinions to yourself.'

'I'm just saying, it is convenient and I wouldn't put anything past Jax Kevolo.'

'This is your official line, is it, Eddie?' said Commander Kevolo, writing Dram's comments down on a pad.

'No. That's it, Dram, you're off the case.'

The colour drained from Dram's eyes.

'Why won't anyone ever believe me?' protested Stanley.

'Sorry, kid. For what it's worth, I was starting to, but it don't matter what I believe any more. Take my advice and listen to Eddie. He's got your best interests at heart.' Dram Gurdling left the room.

Eddie Skulk turned to Commander Kevolo. 'I request a period of consultation with my client prior to tomorrow's hearing.'

'Granted,' said Commander Kevolo, before adding, 'See you in court.'

'When I showed the prisoner the footage he replied, It's me'

The courtroom was an enormous high-ceilinged circular room in the heart of the Bucket. It bustled with
noise and activity and was monitored by hundreds of
automated cameras. Armed police officers stood around
the edges of the room looking menacing. Everyone
stopped what they were doing and watched as Stanley
entered the room. The two officers who had brought
him from his cell escorted him to a seat next to Eddie,
then stood back.

'There are a lot of people,' Stanley said nervously.

'Most of them are court officials,' replied Eddie, indicating those in uniforms seated in front of a high chair
at the end of the room. 'You don't need to worry about
them. The high chair is for the judge, but as Kevolo is
the prosecution as well I guess he'll spend some of his

time in the main argument arena in front of us here. To your left is the witness box.'

'Who are his witnesses?'

'I don't know. The prosecution doesn't have to disclose anything to the defence in cases like this. We're basically flying blind. Behind us is the gallery where the journobots are contained. The cameras will be transmitting the case into every home on every contact planet in every corner of this galaxy. But you don't need to worry about any of that. There are ten people you need to worry about, and they'll be sitting on those benches to our right.'

'The jury,' said Stanley.

'The jury,' confirmed Eddie.

The main door opened again and the jury entered.

'Let's see what we got,' Eddie said quietly in Stanley's ear. 'Right, a moon dweller. That's good. She should be more sympathetic.' A blue-faced woman took the first seat, followed by four more jurors. 'Three Armorians and a Gustovian,' said Eddie. Behind a man in mirrored sunglasses was a tall woman with brightly coloured clothes. 'A Therapian, that's good.' But Eddie's optimism drained away when the final four jurors were all Armorian. 'Seven out of ten, that's not great. There are hundreds of planets not being represented here, but of course Kevolo will argue that since you are being tried under Armorian laws that this is fair representation.'

'Is that true?'

'Unfortunately so. It's not too late to change your mind, you know.'

In the short pre-trial consultation, after a great deal of argument, Eddie had reluctantly agreed to go along with Stanley's plea of not guilty although he pointed out that under Armorian law Stanley, as defendant, wasn't allowed to speak in court and would have to rely on his witnesses. Eddie had strongly advised him to plead guilty, given the evidence, but in the end it was Stanley's decision and he was adamant.

Everyone in the court stood as Commander Kevolo entered and climbed up to the high chair.

'This court is now in session,' he announced grandly. 'This is the trial of Stanley Bound, accused of the assassination of President Vorlugenar. This trial is brought to you in association with Solar Fruit Twisties, the perfect way to start your day.'

'Advertising,' muttered Eddie.

'Everyone please be seated, except for the defendant and his counsel.'

Everyone except Stanley and Eddie sat down.

'How does the defendant plead?' asked Commander Kevolo.

'He pleads innocent,' Eddie announced.

There was a noisy reaction to this from the journobots in the gallery and from all ten members of the jury.

'Order in my court.' Commander Kevolo's cry had

the desired effect of calming the hubbub. He continued. 'Now, I should explain that I have two distinct roles in this case today. As prosecutor I aim to make it clear that Stanley committed this iniquitous crime. As judge I will decide the most appropriate punishment for him.'

'Objection,' cried Eddie. 'This is a presumption of guilt before the case even begins.'

'Objection overruled, Mr Skulk. Everyone has seen the video evidence of the president's death. It's pretty clear what happened. The prosecution may continue.' Commander Kevolo barely took a breath before carrying on. 'Good people of the jury, my case is a simple one. Stanley Bound was witnessed committing this crime by several billion trillion people watching the president's annual speech. Today I will present three reliable witnesses who will confirm that not only did Stanley Bound confess to this crime, but it was executed with the help of a band of dangerous criminals and that, having been caught, he attempted to flee from justice. My conclusion will be that Stanley Bound deserves the highest punishment available to this court, namely to be put to death.'

There was a shocked reaction from the Therapian, the Gustovian and the moon dweller in the jury, but the Armorians nodded their heads in grave agreement.

Commander Kevolo continued. 'Yes, I realise that this is a punishment reserved for extreme cases, but I mean to show that this is one such case.' He stood up and made his way down to the main arena. 'Before you stands a boy with no morals, a boy who killed our beloved president and does not even have the decency to own up to his crime in this honorable court of law. Before you, good citizens of the jury, stands a liar.'

'I am not,' shouted Stanley.

'Silence in court! The accused is not allowed to speak,' snapped Commander Kevolo.

Stanley felt Eddie tug on his sleeve and he sat back down.

'As the first witness, the prosecution calls Senior Officer Grogun,' announced Commander Kevolo.

Grogun looked nervous as he entered the court and took his place in the witness box.

'Senior Officer Grogun,' said Commander Kevolo, 'please state your job and the role you played in the arrest of Stanley Bound.'

'I am a senior Armorian Intergalactic Police Officer and, before my promotion, I was the arresting officer of Stanley Bound.'

'A loyal representative of the long arm of the law. Thank you.' Commander Kevolo rested a hand on the bar between the two of them. 'And tell me, did the accused put up any resistance when you arrested him?'

'No, he gave himself up without a struggle.'

Commander Kevolo smiled at the jury. 'And did you at any stage confront Stanley with footage of his crime?'

'I did, yes.' For the first time, Officer Grogun glanced at Stanley.

'And what did he say when you did this?'

'Do you mind if I check my notes?'

'Not at all. Take your time, *Senior* Officer Grogun,' said Kevolo.

Grogun pulled out an electronic notebook and scrolled through it. 'When I showed the prisoner the footage he replied, *It's me.*'

'But I meant that . . .' began Stanley.

Eddie placed a hand on his arm. 'Please stay quiet. We'll have our turn.'

'Aha.' Commander Kevolo raised a finger. 'There you have it, good people of the jury. When the accused was shown the footage of this heinous crime he responded with the telling words *It's me*. Thank you, Senior Officer Grogun. Mr Skulk, your witness.'

Eddie stood up and Commander Kevolo returned to his high chair. Eddie made a complete circle before he spoke, smiling at the jury, the gallery and the countless cameras that filled the court. Stanley imagined that it all looked very dramatic on the coverage being shown in homes across the galaxy.

'Senior Officer Grogun, after my client uttered the words *It's me*, what happened next? You may consult your notes if you wish.'

'I asked him whether that was a confession,' replied Grogun.

'And?'

'He said no.'

'There we are then. You see, Stanley merely meant that the murderer of President Vorlugenar looked like him, a fact that we will not be disputing.'

'Objection. Conjecture,' said Commander Kevolo. 'Objection sustained,' he answered himself. 'Strike the last statement from the records. The jury will consider only facts and not get distracted by products of Mr Skulk's fantastical imagination.'

Eddie looked temporarily thrown by this, but he quickly composed himself. 'Tell me, Senior Officer Grogun, did the defendant seem aware of who the President of Armoria was when you arrested him?'

'Well, funnily enough, no,' admitted Grogun, 'but then he didn't seem to know much about anything. He claimed never to have heard of Armoria or even the basic workings of cutspace. And he wasn't wearing a translating tag.'

There was a murmur of amusement amongst the jury.

'So, to sum up, you arrested Stanley on a pre-contact planet on the other side of the universe for the murder of a president he had not heard of, using methods such as cutspace, of which he was unaware?'

Before Grogun could respond, Commander Kevolo barked, 'Objection. Counsel is leading the witness. Stanley's feigned lack of knowledge was clearly a trick designed to maintain his innocence. Objection sustained. Jury, please ignore Mr Skulk's last statement.'

Eddie scowled at him. 'No further questions.' He sat back down.

'And what position did Stanley Bound hold amongst this group of violent terrorists?'

Officer Grogun left and a hum rose up in the court-room as the jury and journobots talked in low voices amongst themselves.

'This is impossible,' Eddie muttered to Stanley.

'I thought you were supposed to be the best lawyer in the galaxy,' replied Stanley.

'Even I can't beat a prosecution who also happens to be the judge. He won't let me say anything. This is precisely why I advised you not to plead innocent.'

'But I am innocent.'

'You still don't get it, do you? It doesn't matter whether you are innocent or guilty. What matters is whether we can prove it,' stated Eddie.

'Silence in court,' shouted Commander Kevolo,

causing the noise to subside. 'The prosecution calls the next witness . . . Boosky Retch.'

Boosky strolled into the room and greeted Stanley as though he was an old friend he had just bumped into in the street. 'Hey, Stanley, how are you?'

'Please refrain from addressing the accused and take your place in the witness box, Mr Retch,' said Commander Kevolo.

'How's he going to make this lowlife look like a reliable witness?' whispered Eddie.

'Mr Retch,' said Commander Kevolo, 'please tell the court your occupation.'

Boosky clasped his hands together and widened his eyes in what looked like a well-rehearsed act. 'Until recently, I am ashamed to say that I was a worthless crook. Have been all my life. I come from a bad upbringing, you see. I've been in and out of trouble and prison since I was this tall.' He held out a hand and Stanley noticed that Boosky was wearing his watch.

'And now?' asked Commander Kevolo, with a note of concern in his voice.

'And now, I'm pleased to say that due to your excellent police force I have seen the error of my ways.'

'I see. So it was the long arm of the law which has guided you on to the path of rehabilitation.'

'Objection,' yelled Eddie. 'The prosecution is making a political point. This has nothing to do with the case.'

'Objection overruled,' said Commander Kevolo, with a dismissive wave of his hand. 'Thank you, Mr Retch, I think we all value your honesty. Now please tell me, have you ever met the defendant?'

'Yes, sir, twice.'

'Tell me about the first time.'

'I was here on the Bucket, in the incident room, assisting the officers with their inquiries. Stanley Bound was showing some interest in the posters of other wanted criminals. He gave me his watch.'

'He means he stole it,' muttered Stanley.

'Tell us about the second occasion,' continued Commander Kevolo.

'I was rescued by a vessel operated by a group known as the Brotherhood under the command of a Gustovian called General P'Tang. Stanley Bound was there too.'

'When was this?'

'It was after he had jumped bail, I believe.'

'And what is the nature of this Brotherhood?'

'They told me they were fighting for a universe liberated from the tyrannical oppression of Armoria.'

Stanley watched the reaction of horror from the Armorian members of the jury and court officials.

'Using what methods?' enquired Commander Kevolo.

'I don't know, but I suppose things like assassinations of presidents,' replied Boosky.

'Objection. This is speculation,' cried Eddie.

'Overruled,' countered Kevolo. 'And what position did Stanley Bound hold amongst this group of violent terrorists, Mr Retch?'

'They were taking his orders. They only rescued me after he gave the say-so.'

'I see.' Commander Kevolo turned to face the jury. 'So Stanley Bound escaped into the protection of a militant band of terrorists.'

'That's not how it happened,' protested Stanley.

'I will have order in this court,' barked Commander Kevolo. 'Another word from the accused and he will find himself facing a contempt charge.'

'Is that before or after he executes me?' muttered Stanley under his breath.

Kevolo continued. 'The prosecution has now shown that, not only was Stanley Bound consorting with this soon-to-be-illegal group, but he held a position of some authority amongst them. The prosecution also fully anticipates that, as a consequence of this investigation, further trials and prosecutions will have to take place with regard to the dangerous terrorists known as the Brotherhood. Thank you, Mr Retch. Defence, your witness.'

Stanley felt anger build up inside him. Because of him, General P'Tang and Jupp would be arrested.

Eddie stood up and addressed Boosky. 'Mr Retch, please tell me how many times you have been arrested in your long career as a criminal.'

Boosky chuckled. 'I've lost count.'

'You've lost count?' Eddie raised an eyebrow at the jury. 'Would you agree that until very recently you have been a career criminal who has never shown the slightest remorse or contrition for his habitual criminality?'

'Objection,' barked Commander Kevolo. 'This is immaterial. The prosecution has established that Mr Retch has moved over to the correct side of the law.' Without drawing a breath he added, 'Sustained. Counsel, please desist from this line of questioning and stick to the case in hand.'

Eddie was starting to look worn down by these interruptions. 'Surely the reliability of a witness is of the utmost relevance?' he said, an edge of frustration in his voice.

'Please do not question my authority, Mr Skulk, or I shall hold you in contempt of this court.'

Eddie bit his lip, nodded and turned back to Boosky. 'Mr Retch, you mentioned the group known as the Brotherhood.'

'I did.'

'The phrase *dangerous terrorists* was used in relation to this group, but are you aware that they have never actually been tried or convicted of any illegal activities under Armorian or intergalactic law?'

'Listen, I'm just telling you what I've seen, and I saw Stanley with this Brotherhood lot. They tried to throw me into space. That don't sound so law-abiding.'

'And exactly how did you come to be on their ship?'

'I guess I was lucky. My ship was about to blow up.'

'Lucky. That is one way of describing it. Or did you do a deal with the AIP force to locate Stanley for them in exchange for a pardon for your numerous crimes? You found Stanley because you knew what you would do if you had jumped bail. You would head for a planet outside of Armorian jurisdiction. Isn't that right, Mr Retch?' Eddie said this extremely quickly, managing to get the last word out before Commander Kevolo's inevitable interruption.

'I hope you are not suggesting that cooperation with the police is anything other than a laudable and admirable thing, Mr Skulk.'

'I am suggesting that the testimony of a self-confessed criminal who has no intention of ever giving up his life of crime and is cooperating out of self-interest isn't worth much.'

'Nonsense. The laws of Armoria are based on fair-ness and that includes reformed criminals. The jury will disregard the last comment.'

Eddie was now visibly fuming. 'No further ques-tions,' he snapped, and sat back down.

Commander Kevolo touched his ear and said, 'I have just been informed that we need to take a short break. Just long enough to pour yourself a nice bowl of Solar Fruit Twisties. This court is adjourned.'

'So if, as the polls suggest, you end up becoming the next president, the assassination of President Vorlugenar will have benefited the entire universe as well as your own career?'

During the break Stanley expected the jury to leave the courtroom, like he had seen happen on TV at home. Instead a blue dome rose up from the ground encompassing and isolating them from the rest of the room.

While the journobots made reports back to their studios, Stanley whispered to Eddie, 'We need Dram as a witness. He knows I didn't jump bail on purpose.'

'Dram is a former AIP officer who left to earn more money and now works for me, or at least did until yesterday. Kevolo would eat him alive in the witness box. Besides, the Armorians don't exactly have a high opinion of moon dwellers.'

'What about General P'Tang and Jupp? They know what really happened.'

Eddie snorted. 'Kevolo is on the verge of declaring

the Brotherhood illegal. Even if they were crazy enough to give themselves up, given their role in your escape from bail Kevolo would go to town on them too.'

'But we have to do something. We can't let Kevolo get away with this. He'll arrest Jupp and General P'Tang too.'

'I'd worry about yourself if I were you. This is our last chance. If you change your plea now to guilty I can still get you a more lenient sentence.'

'No way. It wasn't me. It was Kevolo. He set up the whole thing so he could get President Vorlugenar out of the way and take the job himself. And it's your job to prove it.'

'You've seen what's happening. I destroyed both of his last two witnesses and he overruled me on every point. Sometimes when you're losing a battle, you have to know when it's time to change tactics, Stanley.'

'It was Kevolo, and we can't let him get away with it.'

Eddie dropped his head into his hands.

'This court is now back in session,' proclaimed Commander Kevolo. 'To those of you watching at home, welcome back. The prosecution now calls its third and final witness . . .'

'Who's this going to be?' Eddie muttered miserably.

'The prosecution calls Commander Jax Kevolo, Commander of the Armorian Intergalactic Police

Force, to the witness stand,' announced Commander Kevolo.

Eddie was on his feet like a shot. 'Objection. Prosecution can't call himself as a witness.'

'Overruled,' countered Commander Kevolo. 'In cases in which planetary security is at stake the selection of witnesses becomes a matter for the judge's discretion. And, as judge, I deem this completely appropriate.'

Eddie sat back down. 'Prosecution, judge and witness. He'll put himself on the jury next,' he said, slightly too loudly.

'What was that, Mr Skulk?' asked Commander Kevolo.

'Nothing.'

'Good. Then let's get on with this.'

Commander Kevolo made his way across the arena to the witness box.

'That's stupid. How can he question himself?' grumbled Stanley.

'Good people of the jury, I have prepared a short statement which I would like to read to you.' He pulled a piece of paper from his pocket and read from it. 'As commander of the AIP force it fell to me to track down and arrest the person responsible for the murder of President Vorlugenar. This was no easy task but, with dedication and determination, I was able to send Officer Grogun, who you have already heard from today, to arrest Stanley Bound on the obscure pre-contact planet where he was hiding. Now it is my duty to ensure the conviction of this violent and dangerous criminal and thus secure a safer universe for everyone.'

'He's using this as a political platform,' whispered Eddie. 'Look at him, he's looking straight into the cameras. He may as well add *Vote for me* at the end.'

'After the success of the mission to arrest the accused, it fell to me personally to conduct the interview with him. I would like to show the court an extract of that interview now. Court clerk, run the film, please.'

A life-sized hologram of Stanley, Commander Kevolo and Eddie sitting around the interrogation table appeared in the middle of the court.

'Recognise this?' said the holographic image of Commander Kevolo. He pulled out the Damblaster and explained how it worked. Stanley saw himself protest his innocence, stupidly wishing that his hologram would listen to Eddie's advice, then watching helplessly as he took the gun.

'Processing individualised memory handle . . . No adjustment required,' said the voice of the gun.

The image vanished. Commander Kevolo stood up, walked down slowly to the main arena and turned to the jury. 'So you see, good representatives of Armoria and fellow planetary peoples, what I have shown you is that all evidence clearly points to Stanley Bound's guilt.

I have shown that, having been caught, he attempted to escape the clutches of the law and make off with his consorts, known as the Brotherhood. And from his arresting officer you have heard that Bound even admitted his guilt. The prosecution rests.'

The jury looked suitably impressed by this. Commander Kevolo began to make his way back to his high judge's seat when Stanley stood up and spoke. 'The defence would like to cross-examine the witness.'

'What are you doing?' asked Eddie.

Commander Kevolo stopped in his tracks and turned round. 'Do you wish to cross-examine me, Mr Skulk?' he said.

'No.'

'Yes,' said Stanley. He turned to Eddie. 'You have to make them see he's the one who benefited from the president's death. You're my lawyer, and you have to follow my instructions. You told me so yourself.'

'I am waiting for an answer, Mr Skulk,' said Commander Kevolo.

'You're going to ruin me, Stanley,' Eddie hissed, but he stood up and said, 'Yes, the defence will cross-examine this witness. Please could you resume your position in the witness box?'

Commander Kevolo nodded solemnly and made his way back to the witness box. Eddie got up slowly. 'Commander Kevolo,' he said.

'Eddington Skulk.'

'I heard the news that you are running for president.'

Kevolo found a camera to address. He had his fair share to choose from. 'So many of my esteemed colleagues were in favour of it that in the end it seemed churlish to refuse them.'

'And the news this morning said that you are doing rather well in the polls too,' added Eddie quickly.

Commander Kevolo smiled modestly. 'It's gratifying to think that so many Armorians share my vision for the future of our great planet and its role in the universe. I believe that the people are ready for a decisive, strong president.'

'Unlike the last one.' Eddie leaned forward as he said this and spoke casually, as though he was chatting to a friend in a bar, but Commander Kevolo's expression changed to one of deep regret. 'President Vorlugenar was a good man and a great president. We may have had our differences of opinion, but he was a friend of mine, which is why I feel so passionately about bringing his killer to justice.'

'Of course. What I meant to say was that your presidency would be tougher on certain aspects.'

Commander Kevolo appeared to be wrestling between the relevance of Eddie's questions and the opportunity to address a massive audience on his presidential plans. It was clear which had won when he adopted his usual grandiose oratory style and said, 'Although I have always respected President

Vorlugenar, I do believe that towards the end of his presidency he was beginning to show signs of weakness. He had been cushioned from certain realities of the universe. I, however, as commander of the largest police force in the universe, am fully aware of the dangers that must be addressed and the importance of maintaining Armorian dominance.'

'And in your opinion a change of direction would benefit Armoria and the universe as a whole?'

'That is what I've said, yes.'

'So if, as the polls suggest, you end up becoming the next president, the assassination of President Vorlugenar will have benefited the entire universe as well as your own career?'

'Mr Skulk, as judge of this trial I must correct your logic. Simply because I have been forced to react to my colleagues' call for me to stand as president and do what I think is right, it does not mean that the act which caused this is any less catastrophic and abhorrent to me. Now, unless you have any actual insights, I must call this cross-examination to a close.'

Eddie sighed. 'No further questions.'

**'One new thing I noticed was a restricted area. I
thought, why have a restricted area unless
there's something to hide?'**

Commander Kevolo paused proceedings for another
commercial break, after which he announced they
would hear the case for the defence. He laughed as he
said it, and Eddie dropped his head into his hands. 'This
is hopeless,' he moaned. 'Do you know how many
cases I've lost in my career? Do you? None. Not one,
and now I'm going to lose this one in front of the
entire galaxy. Do you know what this will do to my
reputation?'

'Funnily enough it's not your reputation that I'm
worried about. It's the fact that I'm going to be executed for a crime I didn't commit and that the man
who is guilty of the crime is the one who'll be signing
my death warrant,' retorted Stanley.

'Then plead guilty.'

'And be locked up for the rest of my life? No way.

You told me you were the best, and I believed you. Now prove it. The fact that Kevolo is prosecutor and judge wouldn't stop the best lawyer in the universe.'

'If I'd known you were going to be so difficult I'd never have offered my services in the first place.'

'You should have made Kevolo confess.'

'Confess? Confess to what? We have shown that Kevolo has benefited from Vorlugenar's death, but that's it. Besides, I've just looked into that man's eyes and I don't think he's lying. Face facts, Stanley — we haven't got a scrap of evidence to suggest that he had anything to do with it.'

'Well, maybe we would have if you and Dram had spent more time investigating and less time assuming I was lying.'

'The kid's got a point.' The gruff voice came from behind them. They turned round to find Dram, his bright green eyes clashing badly with his blue face.

He handed Eddie a piece of paper.

'What's this?' asked Eddie.

'It's your witnesses plus a couple of notes on what to ask them.'

'I thought I fired you.'

'You just rehired me.'

'I can't do that.'

'Yes, you can,' said Stanley.

'Order in the court,' Commander Kevolo shouted. His gaze was locked on Dram. 'Mr Skulk, please explain why this moon dweller is in the courtroom.'

Eddie looked down at the piece of paper, then up at Commander Kevolo. 'Dram Gurdling is the first witness for the defence.'

Commander Kevolo scowled. 'The court is now in session. Will Mr Gurdling please take his place in the witness box?'

Dram walked across the arena and sat down. His eyes turned an indefinable shade of grey.

Eddie stood up and began. 'Please could you let the jury know your name and occupation?'

'My name's Dram Gurdling and I'm a private detective.'

'And how do you know the defendant?'

'I've been working on his case and I've recently uncovered evidence that he is innocent of the murder of President Vorlugenar.'

An excited muttering swelled in the courtroom and Commander Kevolo shouted, 'Objection. The witness should avoid making statements that he is incapable of backing up. There really is no doubt about Stanley Bound's guilt in this matter. Objection sustained.'

'Can you back up this extraordinary statement, Mr Gurdling?' asked Eddie.

'Yes.'

'Then please do so,' said Eddie.

'Back when I worked for Kevolo I was stationed on the Bucket, you know,' Dram began.

'You are wearing the court's patience thin,' interrupted Commander Kevolo. 'Please get to the point. I won't warn you again.'

'Mostly nothing has changed,' continued Dram, 'but some things have. One new thing I noticed was a restricted area. I thought, why have a restricted area unless there's something to hide? So I checked it out and I uncovered some rather interesting things.'

'Objection. Objection sustained,' cried Commander Kevolo. 'Mr Skulk, your witness has just admitted to the crime of trespassing. This court takes such offences extremely seriously. Officers, arrest this witness immediately. The jury will forget this witness's entire testimony.'

To Stanley's surprise Dram put up no resistance to his arrest. He held his arms out to allow them to cuff his wrists together. As they led him away he winked at Stanley and mouthed the words, 'Good luck, kid.'

Eddie returned to the desk, flustered by the sudden disappearance of his first witness.

'I don't get it. He didn't say anything,' said Stanley.

Eddie didn't reply to Stanley but said out loud, 'The defence calls its next witness.'

Commander Kevolo chuckled. 'Since your first one confessed to a crime, I'm actually looking forward to hearing what your second has to say.'

'The defence calls Professor Karl NomVeber.'

Professor NomVeber entered the room and sat in

the witness box. He wore a benign expression and seemed quite unaware of the stunned silence that greeted him.

'Professor NomVeber,' said Eddie, 'it seems unnecessary to explain to the jury who you are. Everyone is aware of your enormous contribution to Armoria and the galaxy as a whole, but tell me what brings you onboard the Bucket.'

The professor cleared his throat with a small cough and said, 'Commander Kevolo kindly agreed to give me permission to come here in exchange for turning Stanley in. Stanley turned up at my home, you see.'

'You turned me in?' exclaimed Stanley.

'Silence from the accused!' snapped Kevolo.

The professor ignored the interruption. 'I'm afraid so, dear boy. You see, as I explained, I will do anything when there is a puzzle to be solved.'

'The defendant will refrain from shouting out, and I did not give you permission to come here in order for you to appear as a witness for the defence,' said Commander Kevolo.

'What is this puzzle you speak of, Professor?' asked Eddie.

'Ah, well, yes, it's an intriguing thing. Let me introduce you to someone.'

Professor NomVeber reached into a pocket and pulled out Spore, allowing him to climb on to his palm so that everyone could see him.

'Hello, Stanley,' said Spore, waving.

Eddie looked as confused by this as the rest of the court. Whatever he had been expecting the professor to do, pulling a talking mushroom from his pocket clearly wasn't on the list.

'What is it?' he asked.

'I not an it. I am Spore,' said Spore.

'He belongs to the species *Gomphus mobilis*. To you and me that's a free-roaming fungus that breeds in the dark, except Spore is no ordinary mushroom. As you can see, somewhat remarkably, Spore has been blessed with the ability to speak.'

'Once again, Mr Skulk, I feel compelled to remind you that if your witnesses are incapable of providing relevant evidence then I will have to ask you to move on,' warned Commander Kevolo.

'I have to say, Professor, that I share Commander Kevolo's confusion,' said Eddie.

'Spore represents a huge leap forward in evolution, which has hitherto been unheard of amongst such species,' said Professor NomVeber.

'A fascinating biological insight, I'm sure,' said Commander Kevolo, 'but exactly what has it to do with the trial of Stanley Bound?'

'Please don't rush me. I am coming to the point. The facts available were as follows. I knew that Spore had never left the Bucket, but I also knew that such development would have been impossible without outside influence, so it stood to reason that whatever did this to him was on board it. That's why I wanted so much to come here. It should have struck me then, the reason. It's obvious really, isn't it?'

The professor paused mid-flow with a look of wide-eyed anticipation on his face. After a few seconds Commander Kevolo said in an exasperated voice, 'Please enlighten us.'

'I found it in the restricted area that Mr Gurdling mentioned. I could have laughed, it seemed so obvious. Of course, the Planner was on board and, of course, that was how Spore came to speak.'

'Officers, arrest this man on suspicion of trespassing,' barked Commander Kevolo.

'Have I said something wrong?'

'You will remain silent during your arrest,' yelled Commander Kevolo.

Two burly officers led the professor from the court-room, which was once again filled with muttering and shuffling as everyone took in what they had just heard.

'Silence, silence!' shouted Kevolo. 'Mr Skulk, you are turning this court into a circus. Both of your witnesses have revealed themselves to have broken the law, and I have a good mind to launch a full investigation into you once this trial is over. Do you have anything else you want to say before I guide this jury to the correct decision?'

Eddie was leaning on the desk, his head low. There

was anger and frustration in his eyes. It seemed to Stanley that he was barely recognisable from the confident, fast-talking man who had accosted him outside his school gates. On the desk was Dram's piece of paper. Although Stanley couldn't read the words, he could see that there was one more line of writing.

'Mr Skulk, you are trying this court's patience. Do you have anything to add?'

'Here goes nothing,' Eddie muttered under his breath before standing up straight and announcing, 'Yes, I have one final witness to call. The court calls the Planner to the witness stand.'

'Mr Skulk, you are turning this hearing into a farce'

From the reaction in the court Stanley could tell that calling the Planner as a witness wasn't too different from a lawyer back on Earth calling a toaster or a washing machine to take the stand. Even Kevolo laughed. 'You are calling an inanimate pre-programmed machine to stand witness?'

'So it would seem,' replied Eddie, trying to hide his own embarrassment.

'How do you expect it to answer questions?'

'The Planner has a language facility, artificial intelligence and a responsive functionality. There is no reason why it cannot be called as witness. In fact, I could quote you a number of prior cases in which robots and machines have been summoned as witnesses.'

'And how exactly do you expect this machine to

appear in the courtroom?' Stanley felt that Commander Kevolo was playing up to the cameras, trying to make Eddie seem stupid with knowing glances and subtle winks.

'Provision has already been made for this,' replied Eddie.

Stanley understood what he meant when an outline appeared in the main arena, as though it was being hastily sketched in pencil. The Planner was being teleported into the courtroom. As the outline gained colour and definition, Stanley recognised the machine from the video footage he had seen while in the police car. It looked like a black photo booth with two white lights like eyes at the top.

'Obviously the Planner is unable to take to the witness stand, but as per article 167 of the exceptional-circumstances clause it can remain in the main arena,' said Eddie.

'Mr Skulk, you are turning this hearing into a farce,' said Commander Kevolo angrily.

'Unless the prosecution or judge has any specific legal objection, I will continue,' countered Eddie.

Commander Kevolo looked angry, but he evidently couldn't think of one because he simply waved his hand in a *carry on* gesture and Eddie turned to address the machine. 'Planner, please could you state your primary function and your basic parameters?'

'My primary function is to maintain and improve

Armoria's position of dominance in the universe through accelerated evolution of its people,' said the machine in its flat female voice.

'How do you do this?'

'I think everyone here is well aware of how the single most important invention in the history of our planet works,' said Kevolo.

'If you'll indulge me . . .' said Eddie. 'Not being Armorian myself, I have never quite understood this fascinating machine. Please continue, Planner. How do you achieve this accelerated evolution?'

'I scan the brain activity of each individual Armorian to discover his or her potential, then I realise this by manipulating genetic components and improving natural abilities.'

'I see, and what brings you here?'

'I was teleported as per Dram Gurdling's instructions to appear as witness in the trial of Stanley Bound.'

'Sorry, I meant to ask what brings you to the Bucket.'

'Objection!' cried Kevolo. 'What is the relevance of this?'

'Let me rephrase the question. Who brought you on board the Bucket?'

Before Kevolo could interrupt again the Planner said, 'I was transported aboard by Commander Kevolo.'

'To what purpose?'

'Commander Kevolo wanted to learn why I had

made no alteration to him when he entered the evolution chamber as a child.'

Kevolo's face reddened. 'This is a private matter. I did nothing wrong in bringing the Planner here. Vorlugenar had taken it out of action anyway. I was simply curious about it,' he argued.

Eddie continued to address the Planner as though Kevolo hadn't even spoken. 'And why didn't you make any changes to this man when he entered the evolution chamber?'

'No changes were necessary.'

'Why was that?'

'He already possessed qualities to fulfil his destiny and succeed as Commander of the Armorian Intergalactic Police Force.'

'What qualities are those exactly?'

'Strength of mind, ambition, dedication to the primary goal and ruthlessness in dealing with enemies.'

Kevolo clearly found nothing to object to in this statement.

'And by the primary goal you mean the cause of improving Armoria's standing in the universe?' said Eddie.

'That is correct,' replied the Planner.

'But that isn't what President Vorlugenar wanted, is it? Towards the end of his presidency he was beginning to talk about loosening Armoria's grip on the galaxy. That's why he took you out of use, isn't it?'

'President Vorlugenar was no longer a component to achieve this goal,' replied the Planner.

Eddie gave this a moment to sink in. 'Is that your belief or Commander Kevolo's?' he asked.

'This is not a belief. It is a statement of fact.'

'I fail to see where you are going with this, Mr Skulk,' said Commander Kevolo.

Before Eddie could respond, the door burst open again and Professor NomVeber reappeared. Behind him Dram Gurdling held a long-barrelled gun to Senior Officer Grogun's temple. One of the jury let out a scream.

'Everyone, please stay calm,' said Dram. 'The defence simply needs to recall Professor NomVeber as a witness to explain further how the Planner works.'

'This is outrageous, unethical, unlawful and against court procedure,' shouted Kevolo. 'All of you will be arrested.'

'Yes, but while I have a gun to this officer's head you can stick all those things in your ear,' snarled Dram. 'And please, no more objections. You wouldn't want an officer to die in front of all these cameras because of you, would you now?'

Commander Kevolo said nothing.

Eddie looked at Dram. 'This isn't exactly the tactic we agreed on.'

'Things change. The professor needs to explain how the Planner works.'

'We've already established that,' said Commander Kevolo.

'Not quite, we haven't,' said Dram. 'Now, Professor NomVeber, what can you tell us about the workings of the Planner?'

The professor spoke with his usual enthusiasm. 'The Planner is, amongst other things, a mind-reading machine, which manipulates living matter using the material from that mind, always with its primary goal as a point of reference. We Armorians have long since called this accelerated evolution as a kind of shorthand. In fact, it is more akin to sudden mutation. We didn't mind being mutated by a machine because we believed it was helping us achieve our potential. Look at me. Would I ever have discovered how to enter cutspace without this machine's help? Probably not. But this machine was not helping us achieve our individual potential as we liked to think. It was manipulating us to fulfil a predefined role according to its primary function, namely to secure and further Armorian dominance in the universe. The Planner needed someone clever enough to discover cutspace in order for Armoria to expand further into the galaxy, so it increased my brain capacity.'

'You're saying that the machine was working according to a pre-programmed plan?' said Eddie.

'Exactly. But when President Vorlugenar began to question Armoria's role in the universe, he became a problem for the Planner. He even took it out of use. Isn't that true, Planner?'

'It is true that President Vorlugenar was acting against primary command,' said the Planner's emotionless voice.

'I'm sorry, are you trying to implicate this machine in the murder of President Vorlugenar?' asked Commander Kevolo, sounding amused by the idea.

'Ask the question, Eddie,' said Dram.

'Planner, was it your idea to kill the president? And please remember that under Armorian law, you are required to tell the truth in a court of law,' Eddie said.

'No,' replied the machine.

'There. Are you happy?' said Commander Kevolo.

Eddie ignored him and continued to address the Planner. 'Whose idea was it?'

'The idea originated from Commander Kevolo.'

A ripple of a reaction spread across the courtroom.

'This machine is faulty. That isn't true,' cried Kevolo.

'Planner, please tell us the circumstances surrounding the death of the president,' asked Eddie, shouting his question over Commander Kevolo's objection.

'Commander Kevolo brought me to the Bucket after I was taken out of service by President Vorlugenar. Commander Kevolo sat each night in my chamber. I saw in his thoughts his notion to become the next president. This desire complied with the primary goal, so I acted upon it as I am programmed to do and made the necessary change.'

'This is rot! You can see that I have experienced no change,' protested Commander Kevolo.

'That's true. Commander Kevolo looks the same to me,' said Eddie.

'No change was necessary to Commander Kevolo's person,' said the machine. 'For Commander Kevolo to become president, external changes were required.'

'What kind of external changes?' asked Eddie.

'Commander Kevolo's thoughts presented a solution to the problem.'

'What was that solution?'

'The assassination of President Vorlugenar.'

There was such silence in the court at that moment that it would have been possible to hear a fragment of a nano-pin drop.

'How can you believe this machine?' demanded Commander Kevolo.

'Because it does not have a facility to lie. To deceive, yes. To manipulate, certainly. But not to lie.'

'This is ridiculous. It is my job to consider every possibility.'

'Consider or fantasise about?'

'Even if the thought of what would happen in the circumstances of the president's death did occur to me, I never spoke or acted upon it.'

Eddie spun on his heel to face the machine again.

'Planner, did you act upon this idea?'

'Yes.'

'How?'

'I could see from the plan in the commander's mind that the assassination had to be carried out by someone he would be able to arrest, so that he could capitalise on his success in catching him. Also, if the assassin came from a pre-contact planet, that would strengthen the argument for furthering Armorian boundaries beyond this galaxy.'

'It's talking about an idle daydream, not a plan,' yelled Kevolo.

'A daydream to kill the president to further your own career,' shouted Eddie. 'A daydream to frame an innocent boy. Planner, did you frame the boy who stands accused today?'

'Yes.'

'How did you frame him?'

'The person who was arrested had to be unaware of the role he was playing and unable to defend himself against the accusations. So I created a duplicate version of Stanley Bound to carry out the assassination.'

'What do you mean by duplicate?' asked Eddie. 'Can you create life?'

'No. Only change it.'

'What did you change into a duplicate of Stanley?'

'I manipulated primitive matter and turned it into a duplicate of Stanley Bound.'

'And by primitive matter you are referring to what the professor called . . .' Eddie floundered.

'*Gomphus mobilus,*' said Professor NomVeber.

'Yes,' said the Planner.

'What is this meaning?' asked Spore.

'There were two samples,' said the Planner. 'This one was an experiment, to see if it was possible to turn a life form with only basic instincts into something which looked and behaved like a more evolved animal. The second became the replica of Stanley Bound.'

'You are talking about my brother,' said Spore.

Eddie turned to Professor NomVeber. 'I'm confused,' he said.

'It's quite simple really. The Planner's main function is the alteration and stimulation of living matter. He had altered many shapes before. It stands to reason that he would be capable of turning a primitive life form into a likeness of another being.'

'But if you created another me out of Spore's brother, what happened to it?' said Stanley.

'Order,' growled Kevolo, but even he seemed intrigued as to where this was leading.

'Answer the question, please,' said Eddie.

'The evidence was destroyed. The replica was terminated after the completion of his duties,' said the Planner.

'What means this for my brother?' asked Spore.

'This machine killed him,' said Stanley.

'The termination was necessary for the plan to work.'

'But the plan hasn't worked, has it?' said Eddie.

'Clearly there were factors beyond my knowledge,' admitted the Planner.

Professor NomVeber scratched his large head. 'I don't understand how you could make a clone of Stanley without first acquiring his DNA.'

'Exactly. Good point. The whole thing is utterly ridiculous,' blustered Commander Kevolo.

'Why did you select Stanley, and how were you able to make a copy of him?' asked Eddie.

'DNA sample provided by Commander Kevolo,' replied the Planner.

'I am adjourning this court with immediate effect,' bellowed Commander Kevolo.

'You ain't adjourning a thing,' snarled Dram, still holding the gun to Grogun's neck. 'I think everyone in this courtroom, not to mention everyone watching at home, is far too interested in this to go to a commercial break just now.'

'Are you all right, Senior Officer Grogun?' asked Commander Kevolo.

'I'm fine, sir, but this moon dweller will pay when he releases me,' replied Grogun.

'Where did you get the DNA, Kevolo?' asked Eddie.

'I do not have to answer your questions,' said Commander Kevolo.

'Having already made yourself available as a witness for the prosecution you cannot refuse to appear as witness for the defence.'

'Oh, all right. I got a selection of DNA samples from pre-contact planets sent by one of my outskirt spies, OK?'

'Which are what exactly?'

'Spies posted on pre-contact planets that report back to us and let us know when a planet is ripe for Armorian inclusion. The Planner asked for some DNA samples from life forms from pre-contact planets. I didn't know why. It just said it would help achieve the primary goal. I saw no harm in it. I had no idea that it would come to this. My only crime is that this machine has used me in order to carry out murder.'

'A murder which was your idea,' said Eddie.

'You can't hold me responsible for having an idea if I never spoke of it or acted on it. I'm completely innocent.'

'The crime was your idea, and you provided vital material for the framing of Stanley Bound. It doesn't sound like innocence when I put it like that, does it?'

'Until a few seconds ago I was completely ignorant of any of this. You cannot possibly implicate me.'

Eddie turned to the jury. 'Good people of the jury, when this case began you were led to believe that it was a simple one. You had all seen the footage of a person resembling my client killing the president. Now you have heard that this was not my client, but a replica created by a machine which was carrying out the wish of Commander Kevolo, using materials provided by Commander Kevolo. He claims to be innocent because he had no knowledge of his involvement until now, but I put it to you that he was both responsible for the crime itself and for the implication of Stanley Bound. The defence rests.'

Commander Kevolo was undoubtedly shaken by what had occurred, but he gathered himself and addressed the jury. As he spoke he began quietly and calmly, building up to an impassioned crescendo. 'As judge, good people of the jury, I should remind you that *intent* is an important aspect of any crime. My intent has only ever been to serve my planet. It seems that many of us were tricked into believing that Stanley Bound killed President Vorlugenar, but this does not mean that *I* am guilty of the crime. I never ordered the Planner to do anything. Imagine if a machine suddenly acted out scenarios that you had only imagined and never spoken of. Would you be guilty of those acts? I work tirelessly for our planet's safety and protection from menaces such as the Marauding Picaroons. The Armorian Intergalactic Police force is the only thing which stands in the way of chaos and, as commander of that force, I am at the forefront of that fight, so please consider these factors when making your decision. And please remember, your task here is to make a decision on the accused, Stanley Bound. Any other decisions need to be put forward for another case and another jury.'

'Even the deadliest of enemies have to speak sometimes'

Commander Kevolo informed the jury that it was time for them to make their decision. The blue dome rose into position.

There was tangible tension as everyone waited for the verdict. Commander Kevolo called a commercial break and then climbed down from his high chair. Eddie sat behind his desk. Professor NomVeber examined the Planner, which was still sitting in the centre of the arena. Spore left the professor and bounced on to Stanley's shoulder. Dram still held his gun to Senior Officer Grogun's neck.

'Worried what they'll decide, Jax?' Dram addressed Commander Kevolo.

'Not really,' the commander replied casually. 'The jury is charged with judging Stanley's innocence or guilt. The most they can do to me is recommend I stand trial, which wouldn't bother me since I'm innocent. I'd be more concerned about myself, if I were you, Gurdling. You realise that threatening an officer is a serious offence? Of course you do. You used to be one.'

I'll give myself up as soon we get a verdict,' said Dram. 'I just needed a way to get justice. I've got nothing against Grogun. Well, nothing but this gun.'

Grogun grunted unhappily.

'But Kevolo can't get away with it. He's guilty,' said Stanley.

'Guilty of what?' replied Commander Kevolo. 'Even if they do recommend putting me on trial, no jury in the land would find me guilty of imagining a crime. What do you say, Eddie? You're the big legal expert.'

'Unfortunately that's true. With a good lawyer he won't go down for this,' said Eddie. 'But even if he walks free, I can't see him getting the presidency now.'

Commander Kevolo laughed. 'You have no idea how fickle the electorate are. The next trial will give me a platform both to plead my innocence and to make my case for the presidency. You can't buy publicity like this.' He touched his ear and said, 'Right, now, best behaviour, everyone. We're going back live again.' He turned to the police officers surrounding the room. A number of them had their guns trained on Dram. 'Officers, keep your eyes and guns directed at moonboy here. He is confirming for those at home that moon dwellers can't be trusted.'

Dram snarled angrily at this.

'I not understand lots of what is happening.' Spore spoke quietly in Stanley's ear, resting on his shoulder.

'It looks like Kevolo is going to get away with it,' replied Stanley.

'Is that bad?'

'Yes. If he becomes president, Armoria will invade Earth and do the same things to us that they've done to Yerendel and Gusto.'

A loud crash interrupted them as an AIP officer came flying through the main doors and smashed against the side of the Planner. From behind the door came sounds of a great ruckus, the cause of which made itself apparent when Captain Flaid staggered into the room with three more officers grappling with him. Flaid was snarling and thrashing and snapping his beak, but he stopped when he saw Commander Kevolo.

'Ah, Jax, how are you?'

With one eye on a camera, Kevolo said, 'What's this? Captain Flaid, the most feared of the Marauding Picaroons, commander of the dreaded *Black Horizon*, responsible for spreading fear throughout the galaxy, brought to his knees by my officers of the law. Well done. You see, the firm hand of the law has once again triumphed.'

There was a small smattering of applause from the court officials.

'Lovely speech, Jax,' said Captain Flaid. 'I've seen the error of me ways. I lost me ship, you see. That's the thing with marauding. You never know who's going to stab you in the back, so I was defenceless when these officers discovered me. I'll happily give you information that might help you capture those miserable marauders, so long as I gets my fair trial, if you gets my meaning, Jax.'

'You shall be held accountable for those you have killed and robbed, but your candour with certain information and discretion in other areas will be taken into account.'

Stanley noticed Commander Kevolo wink very subtly at Captain Flaid.

'No,' he shouted.

Eddie looked worried. 'Stanley, don't do anything to damage your position now. This is none of your business.'

'Yes, you'll keep quiet if you know what's good for you,' said Commander Kevolo.

'I will not,' said Stanley. 'I was on Flaid's ship when you spoke to each other. I know that you've been speaking to each other for ages.'

'Even the deadliest of enemies have to speak sometimes,' said Commander Kevolo.

'Then give your word now that Captain Flaid will

receive his right and proper punishment,' insisted Stanley.

'Of course he will. He will answer for the terror he has inflicted on this galaxy.'

'I don't believe you. I overheard you talking. You've been doing deals with the picaroons.'

'I've never heard such rot. I would never align myself with such a filthy criminal,' said Commander Kevolo. Again he turned to one of the many cameras hovering nearby. 'This boy is clearly deluded. Tell me, Captain Flaid, has young Stanley ever been on board your ship as he claims?'

'I've never laid eyes on him before today,' replied Captain Flaid.

'You see.' Commander Kevolo grinned triumphantly.

'He's just saying that to get paid. I bet Kevolo won't even put Flaid in jail.'

'Stanley, once again I feel compelled to issue a word of warning,' said Eddie anxiously.

'We didn't believe Stanley last time,' said Dram.

'Well, this time a machine isn't going to help us out,' retorted Eddie.

'Or maybe it will,' said Professor NomVeber. 'After all, the Planner has looked inside the commander's mind.'

'I forbid any further contact with the Planner. It is no longer in the witness stand. Anything you say will not count as legal evidence,' cried Commander Kevolo.

'Who cares about legal evidence?' said Stanley. 'I'm not a lawyer. I'm just someone asking a question in front of . . . how many millions of people would you say are watching now?'

'Guards, arrest these people,' bellowed Commander Kevolo.

'I've still got your officer held captive,' said Dram. 'Procedure dictates that you do nothing until his safety is secured.'

'Never mind that. Arrest these people,' bellowed Commander Kevolo.

'Planner, did Commander Kevolo have contact with Captain Flaid prior to today?' asked Stanley.

The officers awaited the reply.

'Yes,' said the Planner.

'Why?'

'Commander Kevolo was paying Captain Flaid to spread terror so he could justify an increase in the AIP force. This was in line with the primary command.'

'I applaud the girl's spirit, but I'd kill him in a second'

The events that followed the Planner's revelation happened so quickly that it had TV pundits all over the galaxy watching the footage over and over, trying to unravel exactly what had occurred.

The viewers watching live saw a scuffle, a flash of light and an explosion, which momentarily caused a loss of picture. Various voices were heard shouting before the picture reappeared. The eventual analysis revealed that the explosion was caused by Commander Kevolo grabbing a gun from a nearby officer and shooting the Planner. Meanwhile, Captain Flaid took the opportunity to wrest himself free of his captors and grab the Damblaster that had been used as evidence against Stanley.

'Drop your gun, Kevolo,' shouted Dram, releasing

Grogun and pointing his own weapon at the commander.

Instead of replying to Dram, Kevolo turned to Flaid. 'Captain Flaid, I'll pay you what we agreed if you help me out of here,' he said.

'You got yourself a deal.' Captain Flaid grabbed Stanley and held the barrel of the gun against his temple. 'Lower your weapon, detective, unless you want this one dead,' he warned.

Dram lowered his gun, and Captain Flaid dragged Stanley to Kevolo's side. The officers who had been standing around the room had drawn their weapons but seemed unsure who to point them at.

'AIP officers,' cried Officer Grogun, 'Commander Kevolo has betrayed us all. As senior officer I order you not to let him escape.'

'Officers, I am still your commander,' retorted Kevolo. 'And besides, everyone who helps me get out of this courtroom and off this Bucket in one piece will be richly rewarded. And I mean richly.'

One by one the Yeren walked over to Kevolo's side of the room until all of the guns were pointing at Dram.

Eddie, Grogun and Professor NomVeber had sensibly moved out of the way of the door. The court officials cowered on the other side of the room. The journobots watched from the gallery. The jury remained hidden and safe inside their blue bubble.

With his back to the main door, Dram didn't see what caused Commander Kevolo's expression to darken, but everybody else saw the door open to reveal a man with a thick moustache and mirrored sunglasses, flanked by a small army, all carrying guns and wearing matching blue uniforms.

'Jax Kevolo, too long have you got away with your double dealings. I am General P'Tang of the Goodship *Gusto* and we are the Brotherhood, here to liberate the galaxy from the oppressive shadow of Armoria.'

General P'Tang, Jupp and the other members of the Brotherhood took their places alongside Dram.

'Get out of my way,' ordered Commander Kevolo.

'No. This is our day of liberation, not yours. Release Brother Bound and lower your weapons,' replied General P'Tang.

'I've got a better idea,' said Captain Flaid. 'Why don't you gets out of our way, elsewise I'll pull this trigger and spread your little friend's guts across this courtroom.'

'He will do it,' warned Kevolo. 'So get out of our way or I shall be forced to order these officers to open fire.'

General P'Tang surveyed the line of police officers. 'We cannot win this stand-off, brothers. The picaroon will kill Stanley if we do anything.'

'No,' said Jupp. 'Stand your ground, Brotherhood. Flaid won't kill Stanley.'

'Jupp, Flaid is a cruel and unpredictable criminal. You don't know what he's capable of,' said General P'Tang.

'Yes, I do, because if Stanley is smart he'll follow my advice and in about ten seconds make use of the fact that Captain Flaid is distracted, whack him in the beak and take cover.'

Flaid laughed. 'I applaud the girl's spirit, but I'd kill him in a second.'

'No, you won't. For one, that Damblaster should never be used at such close range. Shoot Stanley and you'll most likely obliterate yourself too.'

'Maybe I'm crazy enough to take the risk,' said Flaid.

'Even if you were, it wouldn't matter since the gun isn't loaded – otherwise the red light would be on.'

'What?' Flaid lifted the gun to look at it.

'Now!' shouted Jupp.

Stanley sent an elbow into Flaid's chest and head-butted him in the beak. Flaid recoiled and Stanley took advantage of his loosened grip to free himself. Hearing Jupp yell, 'Take cover,' he dived under a desk.

A cacophony of noise and flashes of light filled the room as both sides opened fire. Screams could be heard through the smoke which rose up from the guns. Through the thin mist this created, Stanley could see more members of the Brotherhood moving into the room.

'Brothers, hold your fire,' yelled General P'Tang. 'Commander Kevolo, you are trapped. We do not want to kill any of your officers. We have no quarrel with the Yeren, but we will do whatever is necessary to bring you to justice.' The general shouted this from behind the blue dome. On the floor lay various bodies of those caught in the crossfire, wearing both Brotherhood and AIP uniforms.

'Do not be fooled by these criminals, officers. Kill them,' Kevolo responded.

'Hold your fire. One of your own wishes to address you,' shouted General P'Tang.

Curlip, the Yeren Stanley had met on board the *Gusto*, stepped into the room. He held both hands in the air to show he was unarmed.

'Brother Yeren,' he cried, 'many of you will have heard of me. Some of you will know my family back on our beautiful home planet. Some of you may even be related to me. My name is Curlip. I am the one who refused to join the AIP force and went to seek a better future for our noble race.'

'Leaving the rest of us to pay our planet's debt,' shouted one of the officers.

A few of the others grunted in agreement.

'None of you should have to pay this debt. This debt is not legal,' replied Curlip. 'If you lay down your guns now and allow us to arrest Commander Kevolo, we can ensure that he is tried for his crimes by an independent interplanetary court. Kevolo has turned our people into a strong army, the biggest in the galaxy, but instead of fighting for ourselves we fight for him, while he holds the galaxy to ransom and plans to invade ever more planets.'

'Why should we trust you?' asked another officer.

'Because Kevolo has already proved himself untrustworthy.' This reply didn't come from Curlip. It was Officer Grogun, who stepped out from where he had been hiding and spoke. 'He was happy for me to die in order to save his own skin. He has been doing deals with the picaroons. He plotted Vorlugenar's death.'

Curlip turned to Grogun and reached out a hand. Grogun took it and they held their arms up in a sign of unity.

'Don't listen to these traitors,' said Commander Kevolo.

'You are the traitor,' said an officer.

'I order you to honour your vows and protect your commander,' insisted Kevolo.

Every Yeren was facing him now. All it took was for them to raise their guns for him to see that he was surrounded and realise that it was over.

'Drop your weapon, Jax,' said Grogun.

Commander Kevolo reluctantly complied with this order.

As they started to lead him away, the blue sphere sank back into the ground and the jury reappeared. They looked around the courtroom in confusion.

'We'll explain later. What's your verdict?' asked Eddie.

'We find Stanley Bound innocent on all charges and recommend Commander Kevolo stand trial,' replied the chief juror.

'I want to go home'

Once it became obvious that the fighting was over, the journobots swooped down from the gallery where they had been hiding, desperate for an interview with Commander Kevolo.

'*Good Morning, Galaxy.* Will you still be running for president in view of the recent revelations of your dealings with the Marauding Picaroons?'

'*Stars of the Universe.* How do you feel about Stanley Bound's role in your arrest?'

'*What Spacecraft?* How do you rate the steering on the new model AIP shuttle?'

'No comment,' was the only reply Kevolo made as he was led out of the hall, stepping around the bodies killed in the gunfight.

The journobots flew across the room and surrounded

Stanley, shoving cameras and microphones in his face.

'*Galaxy News*. How does it feel to be found innocent?'

'*News Nova*. How did you survive on board the *Black Horizon*?'

'*The Salon Channel*. What hair products do you use?'

Stanley was in no mood to answer any of their questions so he was glad when Jupp appeared and fired a warning blast from her gun to ward them off. They quickly moved on to General P'Tang, who was taking the opportunity to deliver one of his speeches.

'Many of our brothers fell today, but their deaths will not be in vain. For today we struck the first blow for freedom . . .' he was saying.

'What happened to Captain Flaid?' Stanley asked Jupp.

'He must have escaped. He's not amongst the wounded,' replied Jupp. 'Where's Spore?'

'I here,' said a voice from Stanley's pocket. 'I not understand much of this.'

'Nor me, but I'm glad you're safe,' said Stanley.

'The machine killed my brother?'

'Yes,' said Stanley.

'This makes me sad.'

'Lots of people have died today,' said Jupp, looking around at the scene of devastation. 'The *Gusto* is going to be a quieter place when we get back there.' She sounded upset.

'I'm sorry,' said Stanley.

'They died for the cause. Everyone knew the risks.'

'Thanks for coming. I know how dangerous it was.'

'We came because we believed you when you said you didn't do it, and, watching the trial on TV, Dad decided that it was finally time to do something. He made a speech about it first, of course, and then we got here as quickly as we could.'

'What will happen to the Brotherhood now?' Stanley asked.

'I don't know, but this won't stop Armoria being like it is. We can only hope that the next president will be more like Vorlugenar than Kevolo.'

'I thought you were pleased that Vorlugenar was dead.'

'I think we were so busy thinking that everything about Armoria was bad that we couldn't see that the president was trying to make things better. Quil was right – he was a good man. He didn't deserve to die, and I'm glad it wasn't you that killed him.'

'Me too.'

They hugged. Stanley felt exhausted and relieved and utterly overwhelmed.

'Well done, Stanley,' said Eddie as he and Dram joined them. 'I think I'm going to come out of this rather well. After winning this case I'm going to be flooded with clients.' He took Stanley's hand and shook it, then pulled him close and whispered in his ear, 'If anyone asks, I always knew you were innocent, OK?'

Stanley extracted his hand and offered it to Dram, whose eyes were glowing yellowy orange like a sunset. 'Thank you so much. If it wasn't for you . . .' he began.

'Listen, don't mention it, kid. I'm just glad we got the right verdict.'

Over his shoulder, Stanley saw that General P'Tang had finished speaking and that Professor NomVeber was answering the journobots' questions.

General P'Tang came over to join them, Grogun and Curlip by his side.

'You had better get going,' said Grogun. 'The AIP is without a leader for the moment, but as soon as they assign a new stand-in commander we'll be ordered to hold you for questions.'

'Won't you join us?' said Curlip.

'No. Kevolo was out of order, but I still have a job to do. It's a matter of honour.'

'We have different ideas about honour, but I respect your decision.'

'What about you, Stanley?' said General P'Tang. 'Will you join us?'

'Yes, come with us,' said Jupp.

'Where are you going?' asked Stanley.

'Wherever you want,' she replied.

'I want to go home.' The words poured out of his mouth without him thinking about them. He had had no idea until that moment how strong the desire to return was, but suddenly it felt like the truest thing he had ever said. He didn't know if he wanted to go back to Earth for ever, but the moments he had experienced when he thought he could never return had made him realise that he wanted to go back there now.

'If that is your wish, we will take you,' replied General P'Tang.

PART FIVE

There is a moment of silence after Stanley concludes his story. It seems to take DI Lockett a while to realise that he has finished. Eventually a small cough from PC Ryan awakes her from her trance. She looks up at Stanley and says, 'And the Brotherhood brought you back here?'

'Yes.'

'Did the Goodship Gusto land on earth?'

'No, they teleported me here.'

DI Lockett remembers how he was covered in dust when he was picked up.

'What about Spore?' she asks.

PC Ryan is unable to hide his embarrassment at these questions, but DI Lockett ignores the look on his face.

'I left him with Jupp,' replies Stanley.

'Why?'

'I was worried what would happen to him if I brought him here. I thought someone would take him away from me.'

'I have a question,' says Dr McGowan. 'I want to know why you didn't stay on the Gusto too.'

'I wanted to come back.'

'Why?' asks DI Lockett. 'From what you've said, you didn't have much worth coming home for. A half-brother who resents you living with him and classmates who think you're a thief. Why come back?'

Stanley thinks about this before replying. 'My life isn't perfect, but then whose is? Jupp's isn't. She's always on the move, unable ever to go home, no friends her own age. Nor is Hal's, living his whole life in fear. But at least I've got a home.'

'Ah, an important lesson to learn,' says Dr McGowan. 'There's no place like home.'

Stanley thinks Dr McGowan says this sarcastically, but he doesn't care. 'Besides, Jupp said she would look in on me in a few years' time.'

DI Lockett smiles and stands up. 'Well, thank you for telling us your story, Stanley. We're going to step outside for a minute. Will you be OK here on your own?'

'Yes.'

'And if it's all right with you, I'll give your brother a call. I'm sure he's more anxious to see you than you realise.'

'Maybe.'

PC Ryan holds the door open for DI Lockett and Dr McGowan.

'Inspector Lockett?' says Stanley.

'Yes, Stanley?'

'Thank you for listening to my story. I know it sounds incredible and no one will believe me, but it's the truth and that's what you asked for.'

DI Lockett smiles kindly. 'I believe you, Stanley,' she replies.

On the other side of the two-way mirror DI Lockett, Dr McGowan and PC Ryan look in on Stanley.

'What do you think?' asks DI Lockett.

'You want my professional opinion?' replies Dr McGowan. 'The boy has an amazing imagination. I didn't hear the entire story, but from what I heard it seemed reasonably well structured and cleverly put together. You're right – there is no way he was making it up as he went along. It must have taken him some time to invent. There are certain omissions though.'

'Like what?'

'Like why the Planner chose his DNA to replicate. Remember he said that Kevolo supplied the machine with hundreds of samples. Why his? What's so special about him?'

'I don't think he knows why,' says DI Lockett, feeling irrationally defensive about Stanley's story.

'I'll tell you why. It's a question of egocentric invention. The story has been entirely created around the storyteller. It's a classic mistake made by those who make up alternative realities for themselves. It's all about him. Stanley feels victimised and ignored in life, so in his invented reality he vindicates himself of all crimes while also becoming the most famous person in the galaxy. It's fairly standard stuff.'

'So you're saying the story is wish-fulfilment?'

'Exactly that. In Spore, we saw Stanley's desire for constant companionship. In Jupp, his desire to be popular with girls. In Hal, an aspirational male role model. In the court case itself, we see Stanley find himself innocent.'

'That's right,' says PC Ryan. 'Remember how he told us about stealing from school?'

DI Lockett nods. It makes sense. But she wants to believe Stanley because she just doesn't get the feeling he is lying. Even if it isn't true, she is certain that he thinks it is.

'None of this explains where he has been,' she says.

'He's been hiding somewhere, dreaming up this incredible story,' replies Dr McGowan, with an edge in his voice.

'Hiding where? I had half my force out looking for him.'

'Perhaps he knew that too. Maybe that's why the police feature so heavily in his story. Give me some time with him alone. I'll get your answers for you.'

DI Lockett doesn't want to leave McGowan alone with Stanley. She doesn't like the man, but she knows that she must act professionally in this matter. Stanley's disappearance has been big news. As soon as the media gets wind that he has turned up they will descend on the station like hungry wolves. She must do everything she can to ensure that correct procedure is followed. Regardless of her own personal feelings, if Dr McGowan can help unravel the mystery then she must go against her instincts and give him some time alone with Stanley.

'I'm going to call his brother and get him to come here,'

she says. 'You have until I get back.'

'That should be long enough,' replies Dr McGowan.

Stanley is disappointed to see the psychologist re-enter the room alone. He likes DI Lockett. He is less sure about this man. He closes the door behind him.

'Detective Inspector Lockett seems quite taken with your story,' he says.

'I don't expect anyone to believe me,' replies Stanley.

'Because it's a lie?' Dr McGowan asks it like it's a question but it sounds more like an accusation.

'No. Because it sounds incredible and unless you've left this planet then it all sounds impossible.'

'Let's say the story is true, shall we? There are a few things that bother me.'

'Like what?'

'The spy who sent your DNA, who was that?'

'I don't know. It could be anyone, couldn't it? People leave DNA all over the place: hair, spit, toenails. And Kevolo said he got hundreds of samples.'

'So why did the Planner select your DNA for replication?'

'I don't know.'

'But presumably there was some reason why the Planner thought a replica of you would make the ideal killer of the president.'

'You'd have to ask it.'

'Yes, but that's not possible, is it? Kevolo's shot put it beyond repair, didn't it?'

'I don't know. We left straight after. They'll probably be able to mend it.'

Dr McGowan leans over the table and says, 'No, they can't.'

Stanley recoils. 'How do you know?'

Dr McGowan smiles. Something about him seems different.

'Who are you?' says Stanley.

'My name is of no consequence.' He pulls out from his pocket a syringe with a long needle and purple liquid inside the vial.

'Psychologists don't carry syringes,' says Stanley. He tries to move back but Dr McGowan's hands clamp his wrists down against the table. It takes him a moment to realise but he sees that Dr McGowan is holding the syringe in one hand while using two more to prevent him from moving. He has three arms. 'You're an Armorian.'

'Indeed I am and a child of the Planner, which you helped destroy. Now, don't worry, this won't hurt . . . It will kill you, but it won't hurt.'

'Help!' shouts Stanley.

'It's soundproofed,' says Dr McGowan calmly.

Stanley looks up at the camera.

'PC Ryan has disabled that,' says Dr McGowan. 'And he's making sure no one is looking in through the two-way mirror. DI Lockett won't be able to help you now. And when I've killed you I'll get rid of her too. She seems far too susceptible to your story, doesn't she?'

'But why?'

'I'm a containment officer, Stanley. It's of the utmost importance that pre-contact planets remain just that, pre-contact. We certainly don't want your story leaking out prior to the point when we decide to contact.'

'You mean invade.'

'Let's not get bogged down in semantics.'

'But can't you just wipe my memory or something?'

'I didn't bring the equipment for that, and besides, this is neater and much more fun. The problem is that your story portrays Armoria in a less than favourable light, and even if no one believes you now, when we do decide to contact – whether that's in five, ten or fifty years' time – we want to start off on a good foot.'

'But Commander Kevolo's gone now.'

'Kevolo was one man. Armoria is a great planet that will continue to expand its borders to ensure that the universe is a safe and orderly place. The arrest of one egomaniac isn't going to change that.'

'So I won't tell anyone anything on Earth then. No one will believe me anyway.'

'That's not good enough, I'm afraid. These people are mostly sceptical, but we can't have the details of your little adventure spilling out and ruining our procedure. Now hold still.'

Dr McGowan angles the syringe down and begins to lower it towards Stanley.

'You is a bad man.'

Dr McGowan looks thrown by the voice because the words haven't come from Stanley's mouth but from his jacket pocket. They are followed by the sudden appearance of a small mushroom, which flies out and smacks into his face.

'Argh,' cries Dr McGowan. He releases Stanley as he tries to grab Spore. Spore rebounds off Dr McGowan's face and lands back on the desk. The doctor attempts to swat him, but Spore is too quick. He leaps off the table, bounces head first on the floor, shoots up to the ceiling then back down on to the top of Dr McGowan's head, causing him to lose his balance, kick a chair across the room and collapse.

'Come on,' urges Stanley. Spore jumps up again, bounces on the floor, somersaults in mid-air and Stanley catches him.

Dr McGowan looks dazed from his fall. He looks for the syringe that is no longer in his hand. Lowering his gaze he sees that it has lodged itself in his chest. He holds his breath in fear that a sudden movement will cause the plunger to go down and the deadly liquid enter his bloodstream.

Stanley opens the door to find PC Ryan standing on the other side. 'Where do you think you're going?' he asks.

'If you don't get out of my way I'll scream at the top of my voice and every human police officer in this station will come and find this three-armed alien. Try containing that.'

Stanley steps to one side so that PC Ryan has a good view of Dr McGowan, who is sitting very still with the syringe in his chest.

'What shall I do, sir?' asks PC Ryan.

'Get this thing out of me,' whispers Dr McGowan.

PC Ryan goes to help him and Stanley makes his escape.

As Stanley steps out of the police station and runs he wonders whether he should have yelled for help while still inside, but it is too late now. Dr McGowan will have hidden his third arm.

Stanley squints in the sunlight. It is a bright sunny day, but cold, and he can see his breath.

He knows that Dr McGowan and PC Ryan won't be far behind.

He turns a corner and sprints to the end of that road. He is hoping to get far enough away so that they can't follow him, but he can hear footsteps and as he turns the next corner he catches a glimpse of the two men chasing him.

'Why you joggle me so much?' says Spore.

Stanley has no time to apologise. He sees an alleyway that runs behind some houses. He has never been down it before, but it seems like a good idea because Dr McGowan and PC Ryan are not in sight yet and he thinks he might be able to lose them. He runs down the alleyway. It turns another corner and then to his dismay comes to a dead end. Stanley feels frantic. On either side of the alleyway are high brick walls with broken glass mixed into the cement on the top. There are wooden doors leading into backyards, but the ones he tries are all locked.

They are getting closer. Stanley tries to formulate a plan but nothing comes. He pushes his back against the wall and waits.

In front of him a tiny black hole appears, no larger than a fly but a perfect circle and unmoving. Stanley blinks, thinking he must be seeing things, but in the time it takes for his eyelids to close and reopen the hole has expanded and two cloaked figures have stepped out of it. Stanley recognises them at once as the men who chased him just before he was arrested by Officer Grogun. They have pale faces and dark eyes, which flicker at the sound of the footsteps behind them. They draw long staffs from their cloaks and spin round to face Dr McGowan and PC Ryan.

'Excuse me, gentlemen, we have official police business with this boy,' says PC Ryan.

The two men say nothing but hold their staffs horizontally in front of them, preventing them from passing.

'I am an Armorian containment officer and you are obstructing official business,' says Dr McGowan.

The men say nothing.

'Who are you?'

'We represent the SSS,' says one of the hooded men. The way he says it makes it sound like the hiss of a snake.

Stanley has no idea what this means, but Dr McGowan clearly understands. 'Well, you have no place here. This is a pre-contact planet. Stand aside, please.'

'You have no business telling us our business,' says the other hooded man.

PC Ryan and Dr McGowan step forward and the two men weigh in with their staffs. The four men struggle together, and Stanley sees his opportunity. He runs back the way he came, out of the alleyway.

Two more corners and he can see the sign for The Castle swinging in the breeze. He is surprised to find that he actually feels as if he has missed the place. He reaches the pub, turns and checks that there is no one behind him, then pushes the heavy wooden door and steps inside.

A sad song of lost love is playing in the pub as the door swings shut behind Stanley. Old Bill is sitting by the fireplace, Young Bill stands at the jukebox and Gullible George is on his stool by the bar.

'Hey, Stanley, you're back,' says Young Bill.

'Been to school, have you?' says Gullible George.

'He's been missing, George. Remember? You saw it on the news.'

'On the news, that's right.'

'Where's Doug?' asks Stanley.

'Isn't he with you? He got a call from the station, saying they found you. He left us minding the bar for him,' says Young Bill.

'Listen, this is going to sound crazy, but any second now some people are going to come through that door looking for me. If they find me, they'll kill me. I need to hide.'

'Are you in some kind of trouble?' asks Young Bill.

'Use the cellar,' says Old Bill. 'We'll tell them you went out the back.'

'Thanks.' Stanley nods and rushes round the side of the bar. He lifts up the trapdoor that leads to the cellar and goes down. He has only ever been here before to help himself to the occasional packet of peanuts. There is only one way in or out. If Dr McGowan and PC Ryan have got past the men in cloaks, they will come to the pub. He knows that the Bills won't give him away and he can only hope that George doesn't say anything stupid. If they do find him he has nowhere to run.

He watches the cracks of light round the cellar door and listens to the footsteps. Someone has entered the pub. He hears two thuds like two heavy sacks being dropped on the floor. Or like two bodies collapsing.

'I scared,' says Spore.

Stanley puts his hand over Spore's mouth to prevent him saying any more. He is scared too. The crack in the trapdoor widens. It is being opened from above.

PC Ryan's voice says, 'Come on up, we know you're down there. You don't want to die like a rottleblood in a cellar, do you now?'

Stanley walks up the steps. As he nears the top PC Ryan grabs his collar and drags him round the other side of the bar. He sees Young Bill and George lying unconscious on the floor. Dr McGowan is standing next to Old Bill.

'Don't worry, they're not dead,' says Dr McGowan.

'We don't want to cause any more deaths than necessary,' says Old Bill.

'Old Bill? You're the spy?' says Stanley incredulously.

'Yes, and I've been stuck on this miserable planet for fifteen years. I'm glad I'll have to finally leave, but, do you know, I've come to quite like those two. I liked you too, Stanley, but this is my job. You understand, don't you?'

'No, I don't understand.'

'Sorry, were you hoping a spy would be a bit more glamorous? To be honest, I was hoping for a bit more glamour myself. Instead I've just been stuck here, sending reports back on you lot.'

'So you sent Kevolo my DNA?'

'I sent him lots of people's DNA. After the request came down, I simply hung on to one strand of hair from every head I cut, bundled it up and sent it to Kevolo. Suddenly this stupid job I'd got of trimming your head growths became useful. I figured they just wanted it for some kind of species analysis. I'd forgotten yours was even amongst them, and I certainly couldn't have guessed it had anything to do with the murder of President Vorlugenar.'

'And it was you that led them here to arrest me?'

'Yes. When I saw you on the interplanetary news I figured that there was more to you than I realised.'

'Good, good. Now he knows why he's going to die.' Dr McGowan interrupts. 'Let's get on with this, shall we, before we encounter any more problems?'

'What happened to those men in the alley?' asks Stanley, trying to keep them talking.

'Your friends from the SSS won't be bothering us again.' Dr McGowan lifts up his syringe to show that the plunger has been pushed down.

'What's the SSS?'

'The Secret Society of Steppers. I have no idea why they were trying to protect you. Now, PC Ryan, it's time to finish this. I've used up my poison. What else do we have to kill him with?'

PC Ryan pulls a gun from his holster. 'I found this in that police station. It's a primitive weapon but it's taken enough lives on this planet and it'll serve our purpose. Plus it means that we won't need to dispose of the body. It won't look suspicious. It will look like any other ordinary Earth-bound murder.'

'I will not let you kill Stanley.' Spore leaps out of Stanley's pocket but PC Ryan is too quick and bats him away with the side of the gun. Spore smashes into a half-empty pint glass and disappears behind the bar.

'Hide, Spore,' says Stanley.

'We'll get him in a minute,' says Dr McGowan. 'Now, let's end this.'

'Sorry, Stanley. As I say, it's nothing personal,' says Old Bill.

PC Ryan undoes the safety catch and points the gun at Stanley's chest. After everything he has been through, it will be an ordinary bullet from an ordinary gun that kills him. Of all the places he has visited, he will die in the bar where he has spent his whole life.

'Hold on. It will be cleaner if the spy shoots him,' says Dr McGowan.

'That's not in my job description,' says Old Bill.

'People know you here, and the two we've knocked out will testify that it was you. If you kill the boy, the police will search for you, and since you'll be coming back with us they'll never find you. It's much neater.'

'Oh, all right.' Old Bill takes the gun and points it at Stanley's chest.

Stanley thinks about Doug returning to the pub, probably angry that he wasn't at the police station. He imagines him opening the pub door to find his dead body. He thinks about DI Lockett, whom they also plan to kill. He imagines Lance Martin going on TV again to talk about what great friends they were. He thinks about how he will never get to go back to space, and that he will never see Jupp or Hal again. The thoughts swirl about in his mind and he feels sad and frustrated and scared, but it is anger which focuses his eyes. He sees a small black dot, the size of a pinprick, in the air in front of him. He looks up at Old Bill, who is squeezing the trigger of the gun.

He doesn't know how or why, but he understands perfectly what the black dot is. He claps his hands at the same moment that the gun makes a bang. He steps forward as the bullet flies from the barrel, but the bullet doesn't make impact. It hits a bottle of whisky and embeds itself in the far wall. The three men look at each other in utter confusion. Stanley has gone.

Stanley doesn't see any of this. He is no longer standing in the pub. He is no longer on Earth. He is no longer anywhere. He has made his first step. The pastel colours of cutspace dance around him and he realises that this is why the Planner chose his DNA. This is how his replica got past the security. He remembers being told that steppers make the best criminals. He is not a criminal, but he is a stepper. He can go anywhere from this point. It is a good feeling.

The End